INFINITE MINE

L'VE HALL

Infinite Mine. Copyright © 2020 by L'Ve Hall

For permission requests, please contact (Essential Daze & Co./Beheard@essentialdazeco.com). and/or (Author L'Ve Hall/shauntadah2@gmail.com)

ISBN: 978-1-7350481-3-0

E-Book ISBN: 978-1-7350481-4-7

First paperback edition September 2020.

Edited by B.Edits

Cover Art by Uniquely Tailored

Printed by Book Baby Book Printing in the USA.

About the Author

Shaun Cochran-Hall created the life of her dreams. Surrounded by her treasured husband, fierce daughters and adored grandkids, there's no limit to her achievements. She forged her life's path through education and determination. Many who have had the pleasure of meeting her will say her natural way of "slaying the day" is easily passed on to you. You feel just as unstoppable and inspired in her presence. Shaun's passion for the artistry of writing permeates throughout her soul like her favorite, crisp glass of Moscato. She has written several novels and considers her writing a hobby of habit. Infinite Mine is the first of her many novels to be published and embodies her unuttered dreams of being a writer. When she isn't writing, you can find her spending time with family, finding a fly pair of stiletto heels, or stepping out with her fellow sorority sisters. She currently resides in Las Vegas, NV, with her heart always planted in Detroit, MI.

Instagram: @AuthorLVeHall
Twitter: @LVeHall20
Facebook: L'Ve Hall

Acknowledgements

Heavenly Father, thank you for loving me enough to give me this beautiful life. Your Blessings will always be my praise! To My husband, Gregory, my five children, grandchildren, family and friends. Thank you for your support and encouragement. I love you. To my critique and peer team, Althea and Heather. To my inspiration and motivators, Dayla, Dayanni, Daynice.
Thank you for your time and input to make this story come to life. Most of all, thank you for your enthusiasm and support. To my graphic artist, Jessica. You helped me in more ways than you'll ever know. To those that knew I had picked back up my hobby of writing. Thank you for encouraging me and giving me the confidence to step out of my comfort zone.

You vowed to give me infinite joy---You are infinite mine… Gregory T. Hall.

Chapter One
ALEXIS

*D*amn! I'm going to miss my flight! I tried not to panic because my alarm was supposed to wake me up 45 minutes ago. It's 6:45 am and my flight is scheduled for departure at 8:45 am. We made it back to the hotel a little after 4:30 this morning. I knew I should have just stayed up. Looking down at my watch, it read 7:35. I'm trying not to panic! The airport is 30 minutes away. My flight is scheduled to depart in exactly one hour and fifteen minutes from now. Sitting in the back of my Uber, my mind was trying not to think about the possibility of missing my flight. Even if my luggage didn't make the flight, my ass had to. I couldn't dare miss work after being on vacation for two weeks. Being away from the office meant triple the work when you returned. Within two weeks, I already had three large audits waiting on my desk that had to be completed and cleared in the next two weeks. Being a senior auditor for casinos in Las Vegas was not easy. The good thing was that I had a whole team that worked under me to make sure everything was done correctly and policies were intact. My team was known as one of the best in the business. Up until now, I've always been considered responsible and the most responsible one out of me and my two best friends. So this oversleeping and poor planning on my part was eating me up at this point. Dammit Lexi, the next trip you have to plan better!

The last ten days in New York with my best friends was a blast and just what I needed. I laughed to myself, remembering last night how me, Jess, and Evelyn had the time of our lives at a club we heard about from an employee at the hotel. The upscale club was brand new and full of new yorkers having a great time. This year, we celebrated our "dirty thirty" so last night being our last night in town, we turned up a little extra! We danced, drank way too much and laughed all night. For me, it felt wonderful to just let loose and enjoy the closest thing I had to family. While at the club last night, we took shots after shots and the next thing I knew was I was on the stage in a dance off. Since I could remember, dancing had always been my thing. I didn't just enjoy dancing, I was good at it. I'm not sure where I got my rhythm and hip movements from but once the music starts and I'm feeling it, I just do what feels good to the beat. I never seem to care who's watching. Evelyn's nickname for me was "rump shaker." She often questioned how I was an introvert and extrovert combined. I honestly think it's a matter of drinking versus non-drinking. Although, I feel like I do have a couple of different sides to me. The best part of the night was that we all left with more money than what we started with because I won the dance off and split my winnings with my girls. When the challenge began, they said the winner would take home $100. I heard the DJ say something about a donation. Regardless, I won $500 just from dancing! First, we got in free, then someone paid our tab off and I won $500. This trip was one of the best for us, and we couldn't wait to see each other again. This morning, we all hugged and cried. It was always hard for us to separate and say good-bye after spending time together. We'd been best friends since freshman year in college and this was our annual girls trip. Although we'd been friends for a little over 10 years, we started this tradition eight years ago, after the accident that changed my life. Our girls' trip each year consisted of the typical girls trip shenanigans to include swapping clothes because we all wore close to the same size. Jess was the smallest. She was average height and slim to medium physique. Evelyn and I were pretty average except my legs and thighs were a little bigger than theirs and Evelyn's boobs were bigger than all of ours. Needless to say, we always went home with someone else's goods. Jess even came with some new music from Jhene Aiko, and we sang the hell out of B.S. all week! I was already looking forward to our next trip! Both Jess and Evelyn were from Georgia. I was from Nevada. We met at the freshman orientation and have been inseparable since. Both of their families were my family. I eventually moved back to Las Vegas to finish school, but we remained friends and eventually, their families turned into the only family that I have.

~

*J*ess was currently working at a law firm as a lead mediator. She's also known as a workaholic. Jess has had a job from the age of sixteen years old and bragged about it often. Being the only child to a cop and a parole officer, law and discipline had been instilled in her at an early age. Jessica Renee Stone was also the apple of her parent's eye. Jess' determination to excel in everything helped her graduate a semester before both Evelyn and I. Once Jess finished up, she came to stay with me as I completed my last semester in Las Vegas. Jess is the friend that knows everything. If she doesn't know, she will find out. She's very outspoken and loyal to a fault especially when it comes to her family and friends. Jess and I are very close. She has proven over the years to be beyond my dearest friend. With her cocoa complexion and athletic but feminine sex appeal, she often intimidated most men. She also enjoyed running at least five miles a day. Her prettiness is on a Cover Girl level. Jess is currently dating a divorced attorney in her law firm, but she hardly ever wants to talk about him or them. She mentions him somewhat now and then but quickly changes the subject. When I am in my petty mood, I ask about him. "So Jess, how is your Boo thang doing?" Like clockwork, "Same as yours, bitch!" I usually say something like "fuck you." and we laugh it off. Jess was notorious for keeping her relationships a secret. Funny because me and Evelyn always knew about them.

~

*E*velyn James Johnson is the sweetest person I know. She is a pediatric nurse and loves her job. Evelyn is married to Rich, her college sweetheart. They had broken it off right after college but reconnected years later and married two years ago. When Rich returned he had a baby from another female, so Evelyn became a stepmom first. I can say he loves his daughter. Maybe a little too much because nothing comes before her to include his wife at times. Evelyn hasn't been happy because she wants kids and has not gotten pregnant yet. Happy or not, divorce will never be an option for her. Evelyn's mother is white and her father is black. They divorced her freshman year of college. She's the youngest and only girl of three brothers. She along with her brothers and their parents are still very close. They all still travel together and spend every holiday with each other. I remember her saying that when she gets married, she would never get a divorce. She believed in marriage and commitment. In my opinion, Evelyn sometimes gives too much in all of her relationships. I see her getting very little in return. For this trip, I packed all sorts of gifts for her to include a whole self spa package. I just love seeing her on the receiving end sometimes. Evelyn's innocent face and caring personality are what most people misread about her. What they didn't know was that she was one tough cookie!

~

*A*bout two months ago, I was sitting on my patio enjoying the beautiful views of the mountains and I just started crying. I couldn't understand why. Thoughts about my family kept flashing in my mind. The crying spells went on daily and always happened when I was alone. I wasn't quite sure as to why all the tears or what exactly was going on. I just knew I often found myself drowning in the realization of how lonely I really was. Outside of work, I didn't socialize much. My daily routine was pretty consistent. I would wake up, go to work, work past my end time, go home, talk with Jess and

Evelyn, listen to music or watch television and then go to sleep. Outside of my standing hair, nail, eyelashes, waxing appointments, and occasional yoga classes, I pretty much was in my condo alone. I thought about selling my condo and moving back to Georgia or adopting a pet, but hadn't acted on either. Whenever I thought about leaving Vegas, the reality of the beautiful weather and family roots changed my mind for me. Over the last month, I started thinking about my past and my future. I started having my crying spells more frequently but I hadn't shared that with anyone. I thought about calling my therapist to see about getting in for an appointment but hadn't yet. My weekly therapy sessions ended over three years ago. For the last week or so, with my best friends, I haven't cried once other than from laughing so hard. I think I just needed to be around friends. Time with them was therapeutic for me.

Also, during this trip, I ended my so-called relationship with Sean. The dysfunctional "relationship" had to stop. I had been messing around with Sean now going on two years. Having him in my life started making me feel unhappy. We lived four driving hours away from each other. When we first met, we had planned on seeing each other at least once a month. Needless to say, I can count on one hand the total times we had spent together in two years. He and I spent more time arguing over the phone and dealing with bullshit than anything. I was constantly arguing with him about why he didn't show when he said he called to tell me he was on his way? Why didn't he call me like he said he would? Why did he ignore my text? Sean was a habitual liar and had been caught in many lies about other women on more than one occasion. He once had the audacity to try to check me about questioning him. He said something to the fact of you can't blah blah blah because we're not technically in a relationship, blah blah blah. Just thinking about it, pissed me off again. The funny thing was that I couldn't question him, but he could question me. I made the mistake of taking him to my office holiday party last year. He was rude and arrogant. In a three-way conversation with my besties, I told them that he must have thought he was all that because he had just bought his first pair of

Louboutin dress shoes. Come up on at least a couple of pairs before you start stunting, Asshole! Long story short, he became all possessive and shit because a couple of male coworkers complimented me as soon as we walked in. That night during a heated argument back at my condo, he told me that he was embarrassed that I wore such a short dress and that I looked desperate. The audacity of his insecure ass. So glad he was officially a thing of the past. I felt good. Come to think of it, he was lame as hell. Plus I always had to wear flats, so I wouldn't be taller than him and I'm only 5'6"! I hate to think that I let myself accept that type of treatment from anyone just to say I had someone. Never again! Looking forward to continuing my weekly relationship with the silver bullet!

Chapter Two
ALEXIS

*P*ulling up to the airport, I had less than an hour to check my bag and get through security and get to my gate. The airport looked like a city inside of a city. This place was huge! I had on a pair of black leggings, a white NYC T-shirt, my black zip up hoodie and some cute new Adidas tennis shoes I purchased while in New York. My hair was in a side part swoop ponytail that hung just past my shoulders. I had removed my clip in hair extensions this morning. I walked as fast as I could without running. I wanted to stop at Auntie Annie's and grab a pretzel, but I didn't want to miss my flight. Security was a little slow but believe it or not, I made it to my gate with close to 10 minutes to spare before boarding began.

I found a seat, plugged my phone in to charge it. I sent my text to let the girls know I made it to my gate. As I was exchanging text messages in our group chat and saving pictures that we shared, I looked across from where I was sitting and laid eyes on *him*. My breathing instantly slowed down but my heart started beating fast at the same time. *Fade to black.* He was one sexy ass dark chocolate man. I looked around to see if anyone else was looking at him or looking at me looking at him. Honestly, his attractiveness was not to be passed by nor ignored. He was dark and beautiful! His skin was so smooth. I licked my lips looking at him. *Damn.* His lips! His lips weren't as full as mine, but they were perfect. His mouth looked so strong. He had his mouth where one side was slightly upward in a smirk and I was instantly emulating him. I noticed how perfectly groomed he looked. His hair was short with deep waves. His full goatee was close shaved along the jawline and thin mustache. As you moved down his jawline his beard faded into a thick, short trimmed beard. He looked damn near edible. His eyebrows were nice and almost connected. He was dressed in all black too. He was wearing an all black sweatsuit, white shirt and black sneakers. He wore a flat silver and diamond chain and both his ears were pierced with small diamond studs in them. He was so appealing and strong looking. I had to look away because I started thinking that I have a problem! He wasn't wearing a wedding band. There was no way a man like this was single. As I was checking him out, I noticed he was checking me out too. We both failed at trying to be discreet. There was at least a fifteen-second stare down. Not sure what he was thinking, but I was thinking... *I hope the flight is delayed, and we have to spend the night here together... Laughing to myself again.* I needed my girls here. There is no doubt Jess and Evelyn would have been all in his personal space and making him feel uncomfortable with their flirtatious remarks and gestures. I discreetly snapped a quick picture of him while he wasn't looking and sent it to the group text with the caption I'm suddenly craving dark chocolate! Laughing at the replies that came back one by one. I looked up, and he was looking directly at me, again. That's when I decided to speak.

"Hi," I said with a slight smile and a one finger wave.

"Morning," he replied with a head movement nod.

He did that crooked smile.

Oh shit! I suddenly became aware of my appearance. I hadn't looked in a mirror since I left the hotel. I hope my ponytail wasn't looking like I'd been in a hurricane. He's over there looking like fine wine and I'm over here looking like a beer. I ran my hand over my head to slick down any hair out of place. I wasn't wearing any makeup and I know my eyes say I'm hungover and tired. Shit! At least I had my eyelashes done. I managed to cross my legs and look as natural as possible. I reached in my purse and applied some lip gloss, so I didn't look like a complete freaking mess. In my opinion, lip gloss always makes things better. His energy and vibe were very strong and my imagination was starting to get very inappropriate as I imagined all sorts of things I wanted to do to him. I sat there until it was time to board the plane. He boarded when they called for first-class ticket holders. I boarded at least 10 minutes later.

~

*a*s I boarded the plane, I looked over to my right and saw him sitting. He was still fine. His eyes were seductive. He was impressive. I hurried on pass hoping and praying he didn't see me. At this point, all I wanted was my seat. I needed to go to sleep. My eyes were burning. I'm sure I would doze off thinking about how fine he was. I made it to my seat which was a middle seat. On top of that, I had a person on both sides. This was going to be one long four and a half hour flight. I just settled in and closed my eyes. The flight attendant must have felt bad for me because, before take-off, she quietly leaned over the guy sitting in the aisle seat and told me that there was an extra seat up front. She told me if I would like that seat she could move me. I quickly said yes and could not get up fast enough. With my large bag and cell phone in hand, I followed her up the aisle. *Look at God!* I thought to myself.

I was pleasantly shocked and played it really cool when he stood up to let me in the seat next to him by the window. Standing by him I realize how much taller he was than me and how nice and built his body was. *Damn, he smells good.*

"Thank you!" I said as I sat in the seat next to him.

"Hi again and thank you," he replied

He looked nervous. I wonder if he's irritated that I was moved. I quickly dug in my purse to retrieve a piece of chewing gum. I needed a piece of gum for two reasons. It helps me when the plane takes off with the popping in my ear and two I was sitting so close to him and I wanted everything to be on point. I wasn't sure if we'd talk because so far we had been communicating with our eyes only. I reached for my seat belt and was attempting to bring it across my waist when he kindly took it away from me and buckled it in the base. I was surprised by the gesture and looked up at him. For a moment I might have stopped breathing and caught my breath. Our faces were so close to one another. I could feel his breath on my skin. I quickly reached up to turn the air directly on me because it got hot, real quick. I was so close to asking him to initiate me in the mile high club!

I put my earplugs in my ear and listened to my girl Beyoncé. She always made me feel empowered. *What the fuck is going on?* I am way too attracted to this man that I am now sitting next to. Maybe I'm feeling like this because I haven't been with a man in over six months. I might have to go ahead and give into nerdy ass Roman Tibitt on my job. Something is better than nothing... right? Wrong! Roman is all of 5'1" and considered obese. *Get it together, Lexi.* I closed my eyes and enjoyed my music. I could tell he was looking at me. The plane took off and I must have dozed off. When I woke up, I looked at my watch and realized that close to an hour had passed. I removed my earbuds and noticed that everyone around me had earphones in and was watching movies, sleeping, drinking or eating. I looked over at him, and he was watching ESPN live on his screen with his wireless earbuds. Damn, he's still fine, I thought to myself.

I needed to use the restroom and excused myself from my seat. Once in the small airplane bathroom, I peed, washed my hands, threw water on my face, and fixed myself up. Once I returned to my seat, the flight attendant came and took our order. I requested a vodka cranberry and turkey sandwich. He requested a cranberry juice and turkey sandwich. *Great! Now he thinks I'm an alcoholic!* I thought to myself. I must have made a face because he did a quiet laugh.

"Are you laughing at me?" I asked.

Shaking his head is a yes motion, "I can't lie... just a little."

"Oh wow! Okay! I held out my hand. I'm Lexi, and I am not an alcoholic."

I had to giggle.

"Okay, Lexi. I'm Malcolm and I don't think you're an alcoholic. I just think you're incredibly beautiful."

I smiled and said, "thank you."

The way he was looking at me and the conviction in his state-ment made me feel beautiful as hell.

"I think the name Lexi is pretty and very befitting for you." He said as he paused then continued. "I'm happy that you agreed to sit next to me, Lexi. I have to confess that I've been waiting for you to wake up, so I could get to know you better."

He gave this cute ass adorable crooked smile with his mesmer-izing lips still together.

"Really? You just said all that to me? I don't think I've ever had anyone be that forward with me." I was smiling ear to ear. "So, Mr. Malcolm, what's your story? Do you live in Vegas? Are you visiting? You married? Involved with anyone? Why are you happy I'm sitting next to you?" I inquired in one complete breath.

"Wow! You follow my lead beautifully and cut straight to the really important questions. Huh? Well, let's do this!" He adjusted in his seat looking directly at me. "My story is I'm going to Las Vegas to do some interviews. I don't live in Vegas just yet. I'm not married and never have been. I'm not involved with anyone and I wanted to get to know you. I also need to confess that I already knew your name before you told me and I know that you just had a birthday and turned 30."

My mouth opened in confusion. I didn't know if I should reach for my mace or run. Malcom must have picked up on my body language because he quickly started talking.

"Relax...I saw you at Club Rim last night with your friends, and I am tripping out that by chance we're on the same flight." He said all in one sentence.

I was speechless.

"Do you believe in love at first sight?" he then asked.

We're looking at each other and I'm trying to process everything he just shared with me. I decided to ignore the love at first sight question because I wasn't sure if he asked it, or I was thinking out loud.

"Wait, did you say you saw me last night in New York?"

"Yes, I did! I was the nice gentleman that picked up you and your friend's tab. I'm not a creep. It really is a coincidence that we're on the same flight." He was explaining, nervously.

This time I laughed, "*uh huh!*"

He laughed too.

"How long are you in Vegas, Malcolm?" I asked.

"I'm in Vegas for two nights. I leave out Tuesday morning."

Our food and drinks came, and we continued to talk, share, laugh, and exchange stares some more. Malcolm told me that he's in the music industry. I told him I was a senior auditor for casinos. For some insane reason, I shared with him that I earn six figures annually and was very independent. I did not let him know that I had a savings account with over $70,000 in it. I was not trying to scare him off already by intimidating him. We talked non-stop about everything we could talk about. Trying to get in as much as we could during this flight. He shared that he really wasn't a drinker and that he rarely used foul language. He lost his mom at the young age of 15. He shared that his mom was everything to him. He explained that he doesn't have a great relationship with his dad, but his dad is still alive and lives in New York. He told me that he was 32 years old and has lived in New York all his life. Malcolm shared with me that when he saw me the night before my laugh caught his attention. He also confessed that he paid for our drinks and the extra contest winnings. He said he never thought he would see me again. He even admitted to taking pictures and a video of me sleeping on the plane. We laughed at each other because I had to come clean about the picture I took sitting across from him at the gate. Our conversation was so easy and just flowed.

Before we knew it, the pilot came over the speaker and announced that we were descending into Las Vegas. We both shared our displeasure that the flight was coming to an end.

"What? Did he say preparing for landing?" I inquired.

"This was the quickest flight ever to Vegas!" He added.

Malcolm leaned over towards me and stated that he really enjoyed our first date. Actually, it's one of the best dates he's ever been on.

I'm at a loss for words. I'm also upset that this flight was coming to an end. I would have loved more time. I didn't like the thought of the possibility of me not seeing him again. I sat back in my seat and turned my head towards the window and closed my eyes. I felt a hand on my hand and I opened my eyes startled. Looking into the most genuine eyes I've ever seen.

"Are you okay?" he asked.

"Yes. I'm sorry. I tend to get a little nauseous." I replied and lied.

"Can I give you my number?" he asked.

"Yes."

I gave him my cell phone, and he put his number in. He then gave me his and I put my number in his phone. I wasn't sure what was going on. But I knew I had not felt quite this comfortable with anyone before. I couldn't quite guarantee it, but I had a feeling that I would be seeing Mr. Malcolm again after all. To the average stranger, we looked like we were together. Malcolm got out of his seat, let me out and followed me off the plane. We exited the plane and headed down to the baggage claim to retrieve our bags. Some big guy grabbed Malcolm's bag. I guess the company he's interviewing for must have sent an escort to assist him. My bag came around and Malcolm grabbed it for me. He handed it to me and looked at me for what seemed like several seconds.

"You good?" he asked.

"I am. Thanks for asking." I replied.

"I hope it's okay that I call you sometime? Probably sooner than later," Malcolm smiled.

"You better," I said, smiled and walked out of the airport door.

Chapter Three
Malcolm

I'm sitting at my gate with my ear pods on and finishing up a call with my best friend Drew who is also my business partner at the music label. We quickly discussed a few crazy females I had to block on my phone and then some business. He was updating me on one of our club promoters. The club owner heard about us being at the new club last night and wasn't happy. Drew was explaining how the club owner was mad because he heard that they had to close the doors to the club we were at last night and how his club lost money not having us there especially on a Saturday night. I wasn't trying to hear it because I had already talked to him months ago about tightening up his security. Drew and I have known each other since we attended college together years ago. We met at New York University during our freshman year and have been riding ever since. He will be joining me with the new team interviews later. We would then fly back to New York the following morning on the company jet. Drew should have been a comedian because he kept me and anyone around him laughing. We were very different in our personalities. Drew was the life of the party and very social. I was more reserved and didn't talk much but listened to everything. Drew had a main girl and plenty of other girls. I just had plenty of girls. While I never talked about marriage and kids, Drew often spoke of getting all his wildness out before he got married and had kids. We both were about business at the end of the day. I can honestly attest to this being the reason our label was so successful and had the top names in the music industry. I owe a lot of the label's success to him and his loyalty and ability to form key business relationships.

Drew Deveraux was from New Orleans and came from a family of success. Drew's an only child and came to NYU to pursue a degree in Business. He planned to get his degree and eventually run his family business. Drew's family owned at least four mortgage companies all along the East Coast. He graduated with his business degree but took a different path. Regardless of what path Drew took, he was going to be well off for generations to come. "Drew, let me call you back," I said to him as I watched her walk towards me. The breathtaking goddess from the club last night was here. I couldn't take my eyes off her. I checked her out from head to toe. She was beautiful. I took a deep breath and watched her walk to a seat. In my mind, she was walking in slow motion. I could picture her with me at one of my functions. I could picture her sitting on my lap, laughing like I saw her last night with her friends. In my opinion, she's probably the most perfect female I'd seen. Even in her black leggings and tennis shoes, she looked sexy. She had amazing thighs and legs. She walked with confidence. She had a designer purse across her chest. I have to admit I was jealous of the damn purse. I wanted to be on her beautiful natural full breast that I had already sized up. She had no idea that I was watching her like a stalker as she sat down directly across from me. It didn't look like she was wearing any make-up, and she looked incredible. Her skin looked like caramel. Last night she was straight up sexy under the club lights. This morning she is drop dead gorgeous. I wonder if she knows how fine she is? She was an average height, with a pretty caramel brown complexion, and beautiful black hair. I noticed she had a cleft chin and beautiful dimples when she moved her mouth. Her body was perfect. She was not thin and she was not heavy. She was an average build with all the right and natural goods I could have fun with and that she would enjoy. I couldn't take my eyes off her. My mind went to places that were very nasty as I licked my lips and adjusted myself in my seat. She was smiling looking at her phone. *Look at those dimples.* She is probably talking to her man. *Dammit! Her man!* He's probably waiting on her fine ass to get to him. That smile and those lips alone had me mesmerized. My jaw was tightening as I took in her beauty. In the midst of me looking at her, my eyes moved about her face and I realized she was looking directly at me. My insides shifted. I was in a trance for a minute. *What the hell!* She spoke and I spoke back. I'm tripping right now. I'm tripping out because I don't do things like this. I never trip on females. They usually trip on me. I didn't stare and gawk like this. I don't fantasize about a chick. I didn't have to. I never hoped nor wished. I usually made a request and my request was met. Her laugh caught my attention last night and today she is sitting across from me and everything about her has my full attention, just like last night at the club. I'm Malcolm Xavier Styles. Known in the music industry as "X".

~

They called for the first-class passengers to board and I stood up to board the plane. My phone was blowing up but I was not answering. It was two different females in Vegas that I'm supposed to see while in town. I hadn't flown a commercial plane in a while and honestly, this felt kinda good! I had taken a picture with a young couple coming through the airport doors but other than that, I hadn't been recognized or approached. I made my way to my seat in the first class and sat down. There were three other people in first class on this flight. The flight attendant asked if I wanted anything. I let her know that I purchased the seat next to me but would like to invite someone in coach to sit there. She told me that would be no problem.

As she boarded, I instantly got anxious. I motioned to the stewardess that's the person I wanted to invite to my extra seat. She must have known I was trying to shoot my shot and gave me a sly smile and a thumbs up.

Within 10 minutes, they were headed up front to the extra seat. I stood to let her into the seat next to me. *She even smelled delicious.* We said hello and now I'm suddenly pissed because I wanted to be on my private jet alone with her. Once we sat down I helped her with her seat belt and found myself very close to her mouth. The things I thought about with that mouth. I took a deep breath because I had to get control of myself. I couldn't understand this strong attraction. I'm around so many women every day and every night. I for sure wasn't deprived in any way. Why was I reacting to her this way?

It had been so long since I tried to actually make a move on a female. I was seriously thinking *how do I approach this without running her off? What do I say?* In my line of work, I'm accustomed to females or *label groupies* as we call them always being around and making moves on me or anyone that they considered a baller. There was no trying to impress or beating around the bush. Everything was straight forward with no misunderstandings. I could usually just give a look and unzip my pants, and they were on their knees in seconds. The most I would say was "thanks" if that. This was different, and I am intrigued, to say the least. Lexi just became a goal of mine. I was mesmerized in her presence and wanted to get to know her. She was nothing like what I was used to and I already knew it.

I looked over at her and she was asleep. What the hell! She wasn't interested! I kept looking thinking maybe she's resting her eyes but then I heard the light snore coming from her. Laughing to myself, I took this opportunity to snap a few pictures with my phone. I even did a quick video of her snoring and me shaking my head. Once I put my phone away. I put on my headphones and watched some sports. I couldn't stop looking over at her and wondering about her and her life. With her lips slightly parted, eyes closed and her head tilted she was still breathtaking. I wanted her to lean on me and sleep. I imagined me kissing those lips. The interesting thing about that is I hadn't kissed anyone's lips in over 10 years. Me being well aware and knowing what a lot of females did with their mouths in my world, kissing just wasn't my thing. I looked over at the beautiful mouth asleep beside me, and I was very curious as to what the inside of her mouth tasted like.

After a while, she woke up but immediately needed to use the restroom. I stood to let her out, and she rubbed up against me. I thought maybe I should go with her. *What is wrong with me?* When she returned, the flight attendant came and took our orders. She requested a vodka cranberry and turkey sandwich. I also requested a cranberry juice and turkey sandwich. *Man...I'm in love,* she was perfect for me. Listening to her talk had me in a trance or something.

"Are you laughing at me?" She asked.

"Just a little," I replied.

She told me her name and reassured me that she was not a drunk. "Okay, Lexi. I'm Malcolm and I don't think you're an alcoholic. I think your name is as beautiful as you are. I'm also happy you're sitting next to me." Great, I made her smile a big smile. I felt like I could look at her smile every day and all day. She was opening up and feeling comfortable with me. Lexi was asking me all kinds of questions and I happily answered. We were having the best conversation as we laughed and got to know each other better. I was really enjoying her company. Out of the blue, I asked her if she believed in love at first sight. She didn't answer and I soon realized that I sounded like an idiot. *I hope I didn't ruin my chances with her.* We started communicating with stares again. *I really wanted to kiss her.*

Our food and drinks came and we continued to talk. I told her I was in the music industry but did not tell her I owned one of the most successful music labels in the world. I didn't want to run her away. I explained to her that I very rarely used cuss words. It was something I remembered my mom talking to me about before she passed when I was 15 years old. I told her I have lived in New York all my life. I didn't tell her that I traveled all over the world and was away a lot. I could never tell her that almost everywhere I traveled, I had a female companion to satisfy my wants. I also neglected to tell her that I spent almost every night out in clubs. I did not tell her that I had a separate phone for females that took care of my sexual needs. I did not tell her that I was a multi-millionaire and hardly ever flew commercial flights because I had private jets. For some reason, I was concerned about what she would think of me if she knew. Better yet, I was worried that she would run far away from me and my lifestyle. I never told her that I heard her laugh over everything in the club and was immediately drawn to her. I watched her from my VIP section in the club all night until she and her friends left.

Lexi shared that she worked as a casino auditor and explained what that entailed. I shared with her that I never met a casino auditor before and felt privileged. We both laughed. She even shared with me that she made over six figures. I smiled and thought to myself how perfect she was for me. Six figures in a year seemed so unfair to be compared to the money I made. I wanted to tell her that I could change her world if she let me. She was so proud and seemed to be an independent woman. She talked about how she works most of the time and just enjoyed being around the house and shopping. She admitted that she wasn't on social media. She did share with me that she loved decorating and was a lover of roses. She told me she didn't really have any family.

Before we knew it, the pilot just announced that we were descending into Las Vegas. We both couldn't believe that the flight was over so quickly. I was kinda upset that the plane ride was coming to an end. I wanted to let her know that I enjoyed our time together. I called it a date. She smiled but I could see her mood changed. I touched her hand and felt something I had never felt before. I couldn't explain it but something was happening. We exchanged numbers and I knew I would see her sooner than later. We walked off the plane together and I couldn't help but imagine me holding her hand, holding her around her waist, and holding her in my arms. Something about Lexi was different and made me feel different.

What was pulling me to her so strong? From the moment I heard her beautiful laugh at the club and the resemblance to my mom's laugh, I knew she was special.

Chapter Four

ALEXIS

I should have hugged him at least. I thought to myself as I was walking off. I headed toward the Uber area, and they headed toward a black Escalade.

"Lexi, can I give you a ride?" Malcolm asked.

"I'm good. Thank you tho!" I replied.

"No seriously. Let my driver drop you off. Please." He pleaded.

Not really hesitating, I went over towards Malcolm and the truck. His driver/escort took my bag and placed it in the back. Malcolm helped me in the truck. He then got in. The driver closed the door and came around to the driver seat. After giving the driver my address, we headed to my high rise condominium.

Strangely during the ride to my home, Malcolm and I hardly said anything but on several occasions, we shared looks and little smiles. What is this feeling? I was feeling something. I sort of felt like we had so much more to talk about. I knew this wouldn't be the last time I saw Mr. Malcolm. At least I didn't want it to be. The looks he gave me let me know that he was interested. This was the strangest most normal encounter ever. I tried to make small talk, but he wasn't talking like he was on the flight. He probably couldn't hear or understand me because the music was playing so loud in the truck. The music did sound good, so I just sat back and enjoyed it. I felt like singing along to the music but decided to just enjoy it. I was happy. As we got close to the gate entrance at my condo, I started to feel anxious. I looked over at Malcolm who was texting on his phone. "Can I give you something to remember me by?" I asked.

He smiled as he gave a look of confusion. Before he could say anything, I had jumped out of my seat and over to his. I sat on his lap and kissed him with my mouth tasting those beautiful lips. To my surprise, he was kissing me back, matching my mood. Our mouths and tongues moved about on each other as if we had been doing this with each other for some years. At one point, I think I moaned and then heard him moan. Malcolm was holding my hips directly on his manhood, and I was holding the back of his head. We moved so sensually as we explored each other's mouths. The kiss went on for some time. We finally separated our mouths and did what we do best...stared at each other. No verbal words were spoken but a lot was said through our eyes as we gazed at each other. Both of us were smiling. The driver opened the door. I jumped out and Malcolm got out behind me and handed me my purse.

"Lexi, are you free for dinner tonight?" Malcolm asked with a look so serious.

"Sounds good."

"I'll be here to pick you up at seven." He said with a gorgeous smile.

My heart was skipping several beats. I went into my building with my suitcase and up to my condo on the 27th floor.

Chapter Five
Malcolm

We just dropped Lexi off at her high rise. I am sitting in the back of the Escalade like a teenager who just got his first kiss with a hard on. I know I'm in Vegas to interview candidates for the Las Vegas Company and talk with a Realtor to look at some properties but at the moment, all I could think about was the next time I see her. She had my attention. Lexi just messed my entire mindset up. Out of nowhere, she climbed on me and kissed me like we were leaving each other and wouldn't see each other again. Her beautiful mouth was all I imagined it would be. Her full mouth was exquisite. I could hardly wait to kiss her again.

Tebow was driving and I could see in the rearview mirror he was amused by all this. I opened my phone and instantly felt a surge of happiness looking at her pics from the airplane. Rubbing my forehead, "I think I just met my future!" I stated. I quickly shook my head fast. "Naw, I'm tripping. I'm not trying to trade in my good life just because I just kissed a delicious set of lips." He did the two fingers to the forehead like he was a captain on a ship or some bull crap. We both just laughed. Tebow had been with me as my friend/bodyguard for the last 7 years. Drew and I agreed early on that we needed security.

AMS Music Label had taken off quickly. Here we were two

young brothers living in NYC, worth millions of dollars, bands of cash, living in million-dollar homes, driving in the most expensive cars, expensive jewelry, and music executives to some top artists in the music industry. In this profession, we spent a lot of time in clubs and studios. We were around a lot of people day and night. People that were looking to get what we had even if it meant obtaining it through any means necessary.

Tebow and Big B are our trusted boys from college. Nine times outta ten if you saw me or Drew, you saw one or both of them. T and B both had rooms at each of our homes. We all consider each other family. Tebow was huge, but one of the kindest brothers I know. He started college with us but had to drop out after our sophomore year to work full time to care for his girl and their baby. While we were in college, Tebow always went out with us and when we started throwing college parties, he always worked the door as security. There was no question when our status grew, he would come along with us. His love and loyalty were undeniable. Everything about Tebow was huge. His size, His hands, His beard, His heart and His presence. Big B was just plain old big. He hardly ever smiled. Big B's family was from the Big Island. He was very private about his personal affairs and was always ready for whatever. You could call Big B at 3:30 am and more than likely he is already up, strapped and at the door.

Chapter Six
ALEXIS

I unpacked my suitcase, started laundry, checked my mail and emails, watered my plants and called my best friend Jess to catch her up on my flight and tell her about Malcolm. Jess and Evelyn both lived in Georgia. Jess lived in Savannah and Evelyn lived in Atlanta. Both had just arrived home as well. Jess did what a bestie would do, she googled him before I could even get his name out all the way. Jess started reading aloud. "His full name is Malcolm Xavier Styles. Most people know him as "X." Bitch! He is all over the internet and everywhere. Oh, shit. This says that his net worth is over 100 million!" She was shouting at me as she's reading. Also, this article states that Malcolm was born on March 2, in NY, New York. His parents are Malcolm Sr and Ann Marie." She started mumbling then shouted, "Lexi! This Malcolm motherfucker is fine as fuck! I'm sending you pictures right now!" She told me that he was not just in the music industry, but that he was a music mogul and was part owner of AMS Music. AMS was named after his deceased mother, Ann Marie Styles. Everyone had heard of AMS music. Some of our favorite artists were with this label.

"Lexi, you need to get Instagram or at least Facebook and stay current in the culture. This is ridiculous!" Jess sent me more screenshots of all kinds. I saw pictures of Malcolm alone. I saw pictures of

Malcolm with several music artists and groups. I saw pictures of Malcolm's chest. Apparently, he's been featured in several articles and magazines for years. "Your date tonight is very well-known. He's never been married. I'm surprised he hasn't been linked with anyone". Jess was going on a mile a minute. "Oooh shit bitch, you about to bump and grind!" She asked me if I was ready to give up some goods, I quickly responded that I ain't never been a slut and not about to become one tonight! I'm not going out like that on the first date. I at least have to wait until the second date. We both laughed and talked for a while more.

Jess continued reading everything she could on Mr. Malcom. Malcolm knew damn near everyone in the music industry. He was in pictures and the same circle with people I idolized. Jess even pulled up public records on him. "He's good! No arrest. No records. He has three properties in his name." I was applying my makeup and rubbing lotion all over my body. I heard everything she was saying but didn't put much emphasis on it. In my mind, I was just going to enjoy this night. I might be exhausted but I wasn't going to pass up a date with this beautiful man who left a sizable impression on me. As she continued to give me information on him, I knew he was out of my league but I wanted to see him one more time at least. For this dinner date tonight, I put a little more into my makeup and appearance.

～

*A*t seven o'clock that evening, I was exiting my elevator into the main lobby. The doorman opened the door to the outside valet and just like he said Malcolm was sitting out front in the same Escalade truck that I was dropped off in. It was a hot July evening in Las Vegas and I decided to be just as hot! I wore a lace rose pink pencil skirt. The skirt had hints of black and gray in it and it hugged my curves perfectly. I wore a satin rose spaghetti strap cami and sealed the deal with a pair of strappy clear heels. I flat ironed my hair super silky with a deep middle part. I placed the small side behind my ear and let the full side hang partly in my eye.

The truck pulled up and Malcolm got out looking breathtaking. I took a deep breath and thanked the gods for his body! Malcolm had on a dark blue silk t-shirt that hung loose but detailed his shoulders, arms and abs, not to mention the tattoo sleeve that was visible on his left arm. He had a pair of dark blue jeans and brown leather Gucci loafers. Even through his sunglasses, I could see his eyes and the way he looked at me. *Sweet mother-of-pearl!* This was a scary attraction.

After a proper greeting that consisted of a long hug and a few feels on his muscles. We got in the truck and drove off. I thought I noticed some people looking our way but wasn't sure. To my surprise, this wasn't the same truck! This back seat was a three passenger coach seat. I got in. Said hello to the same driver from earlier. Malcolm got in right behind me. "Tebow, this is Lexi. Lexi, that's Tebow. I'm sorry I didn't introduce you earlier." We both got in and got comfortable. I remembered the kiss earlier and all that I knew about him and felt slightly embarrassed. I was trying not to look nervous fearing he would see something he didn't like. Malcolm put his left arm across the top of the seat behind me. Without thinking, I reached for his free hand. We sat close to each other and played with each other's hands. His hands felt so safe and strong. This felt so right but I knew he was out of my league. I knew I was a dime a dozen to this man. My biggest fear was being involved with another man who would cheat. I knew his world was that of many women and the last thing I needed was heartache and bullshit. I'm just going to enjoy this night and move on.

We pulled up at the Bellagio Hotel Casino and went up to his suite. The suite was nothing short of spectacular! Malcolm had a dinner table set for two prepared in this huge suite. The hotel room was bigger than my two bedroom condo. I was really impressed with the detail. I understood and knew that he had the resources to make this happen on such short notice and with such grandiose ambiance. The table setting on the patio was so beautiful! He had red roses everywhere. He even had a bottle of my favorite wine chilling. He was listening and more importantly, he made sure to let me know he did.

As I was looking around his suite and checking out the water show from the balcony, Malcolm was directing inside the suite to get dinner set up by the hotel staff. Standing there on the balcony, I thought about how good this night was so far. I imagined this to be my norm, with a man just like Malcolm. Why couldn't relationships just be this easy? I even justified why it was okay to be in a room with a stranger.

"What are you thinking about?" I heard a deep voice behind me ask. I turned around, tilted my head a little and shook it to say nothing. Malcom just looked at me and smiled. *He looked like he already knew my thoughts.*

"Dinner is ready if you're ready to eat," he said.

I shook my head, to say yes. I felt so stupid, why the fuck wasn't I talking?

"Can I kiss you, Lexi?" Malcolm asked, already standing in front of me.

"Yes," I replied.

Malcolm held me around my waist as I wrapped my arms around his neck. We slowly went in for the kiss. The kiss was so intense and sensual. *"Ummmm"*, I moaned as I tasted his tongue. The kiss went on for some time and ended with several pecks on the cheek and corners of our mouth. We shared a few giggles and sat down for dinner.

During dinner Malcolm and I discussed a lot. We picked up right where we left off. He told me his birthday was in March and that he usually didn't do anything big or make a big deal for his birthdays. "Maybe next year, I'll do something special." He paused, stared and waited for me to say something.

"You should. Life is short." I smiled and sipped my wine. We realized our birthdays were exactly two months apart. His birthday was on March 2 and mine was on May 2. He told me about his best friend, Drew. He shared that Drew was like a blood brother and that he was in Vegas too. He said Drew wanted him to go to a club tonight while in Las Vegas, but he had to decline because he had a hot date. We laughed, again. We talked about his day and how he had met with a Realtor and found a couple of properties he really liked. I was able to give him insights on the different areas and neighborhoods. Most of the areas he visited today were elaborate luxury areas. Malcolm shared that he co-owns the record label with his partner Drew and that he has a couple of assistants that help him with his day to day business. He said that they were in town for a couple of days interviewing for the new office here in Vegas.

"Everyone at the label is excited about expanding to the west. Honestly, I'm more excited than anyone. It's a dream come true for us." He shared a few other things like his love for music and how he started his business. I told him my birth name was Alexis Lynn Bell and how I just came off an annual two-week vacation with my two best friends. I told him how Jess was *the speak your mind friend* but the most loyal. I told him about Evelyn who was just as loyal but had just gotten married and was the kindest out of all of us. I let him know how they were my family. We discussed our past relationships. I learned that he had never been in what you would call a relationship. He shared that he had several female friends but nothing close to a relationship. "Are you a player, Mr. Styles?" I asked with a slight giggle.

He replied, without smiling, "I don't think I am. I think I'm very honest and I like what I like." For some strange reason, I liked his answer. It turned me the fuck on!

He learned that I had been in a couple of relationships that ironically ended because both cheated.

"My first serious relationship was a college sweetheart that didn't last after I moved back home and finished school. He apparently couldn't handle a long distance relationship and slept with everyone he could. My most recent probably shouldn't be called a relationship. Whatever we were, wasn't enough, and he too had other females and never wanted to commit."

"When did you and your most recent end?" Malcolm asked.

"Not too long ago," I answered vaguely.

I didn't want to explain that it was just a couple of days ago nor how stupid and desperate I was for allowing him to treat me the way he did. Malcolm told me that his mom had passed away from an aneurysm. She was a high school music teacher. He shared that his mom was his everything and that he tried his best to honor her as best he could.

"The last thing my mom asked me to do was not to cuss so much. She caught me cussing outside with my friends the week that she passed. She told me, the most intelligent men didn't have to curse to get their point across."

He told me that he cussed but not much. He also shared that he visits her at least a couple of times a month at the gravesite.

"I cuss a lot," I said slightly embarrassed.

"I noticed!" He laughed. "I actually enjoy hearing you talk even if it's cuss words, besides you're far from a man."

We both laughed.

He shared that he and his dad had an estranged relationship. He told me that his dad remarried within six months of his mom's death. We didn't discuss that topic any further.

I shared that I was adopted by my parents when I was a couple of days old. They were my parents and the only parents that I knew. I was loved and grew up in a loving home. I told him how my parents had taken me to Asia, Europe and Africa before the age of 10. I also shared with Malcolm that my family died in a car accident while I was away in college, almost eight years ago. I told him all about my dad who was my first love and my best friend. He would never let me walk with my head down. I told him about my mom who raised me to be a woman and to always stand up for what's right. My mom was the strongest woman I knew. There was nothing in the world she wouldn't do for me. I even told him about my little brother who was in the car with my parents. He was only 9 years old. I didn't tell him that my whole world died that day of the accident. I didn't tell him that the four of us did everything together and that I was so alone without them. I didn't tell him how depressed I get.

Chapter Seven
ALEXIS

*T*o lighten the mood, Malcolm played some music and poured me another glass of wine. I had to remind him that two drinks was my limit. His reply was, "I got you!" With that being said, I let him pour me a third glass. I loved the music he was playing. I loved all types of music and so did he. He played Babyface and Toni Braxton. I started dancing and singing. *Ooh, ooh forget you were ever mad.* He just smiled and became an instant hype man. I wasn't able to get him up to dance with me. Malcolm explained he never dances. He encouraged me to keep having fun. *If I'm ever down, I'm going to imagine you smiling and dancing like this. This memory alone will put a smile on my face.* He was smiling at me as he sat and watched. You would have thought I was at the club the way I danced song after song.

"Do you know how beautiful you are?" he asked.

I blushed and kept dancing. Snapping my fingers and moving my body in a swaying motion, I felt comfortable watching him watch me.

"What's your favorite genre of music, Malcolm?" I asked.

"I love all kinds of music. I don't think I have a favorite," he replied.

His eyes were speaking to me. I got so caught up in him looking at me, I tripped over nothing and stumbled. Malcolm jumped up and caught me before I fell. However, I had already let out a screech as I rolled my ankle. I couldn't let him know. I decided to sit the hell down. Malcolm helped me as we sat on the sofa. *I was so embarrassed.*

"You alright?" Malcolm asked, trying not to laugh out loud.

"What the fuck is wrong with me? Shit!" I put my face in both my hands.

"You're still fine!" Malcolm added. I looked up at him, and we could not contain our laughter. We laughed for the next several minutes.

I asked Malcolm for another glass of wine, and he didn't hesitate. We sat and talked some more. Mutually, we both did a lot of talking with our eyes in between actual conversations. I couldn't get beyond how attractive he was. I was impressed with his attention to me and the detail of making this night special. I was loving how he made me feel. *I'm just going to ignore the fact that the wine bottle is empty and I was the only one drinking.* Tonight, I feel so special and beautiful. He complimented me on my looks, my hair, my dance moves and my smile. We talked and got better acquainted for over two hours and it felt so natural yet so unreal. With my legs in his lap, he began to unstrap my shoes. He took my heels off as he rubbed and complimented my feet. Malcolm ran his hands and fingers up and around my ankle and legs so gently. I'm not sure if it's the wine or his touch but I felt myself getting really relaxed. Eric Bellinger was playing in the suite.

We locked eyes and in a deep tone hard to hear he said, "I like you." We moved into each other and began kissing. We started really slow and sensual and within a couple of minutes, we were eating each other's faces. At first, Malcolm's hands were holding my waist then they moved up my back. My cami was out of my skirt as his hands were on my back. The touch of his hands on my skin made my whole body feel excited. I needed more.

My mind and my body were in a fight. My mind was saying, *this is insane, you barely know him.* My body was saying do not stop, this feels too good. You deserve this night and this fine ass man. The way we were kissing and touching stopping wasn't an option. I was totally risking it all at this point. I didn't care either. The chemistry we had had totally taken over. I wanted him more than anything. Malcolm kissed me like I had never been kissed before. Malcolm gripping and touching all over my body made me feel like I was the most desirable thing in his life.

"Are you on birth control?" he asked in between kisses on my face.

I wanted to lie and say yes. But I answered honestly..."No. I've been meaning to get on something." I admitted.

Malcolm stopped kissing me abruptly. He looked at me.

"I have condoms. Are you good with that?"

"Hell yes." I answered.

I placed my mouth right back on his and pulled his shirt over his head. Damn! His chest was indeed a work of art. Malcolm quickly removed his clothing. He stood me up and removed my skirt and then my cami. Standing there in just my thong and Malcolm in his boxer briefs, I couldn't figure out what to stare at...his lips or his very noticeably huge manhood. My mouth moved but nothing came out as I said "Oh shit." Malcolm must have read my lips and my mind because he immediately picked me up and kissed me. I wrapped my thighs around him as he carried me to the bedroom in the hotel and laid me down on the bed. This was going to be worth every bad judgment I could think about. Malcolm was kissing me nonstop and making his way down my neck and beyond. As he devoured my breast with his mouth, his fingers found the hottest part of my body and entered. Malcolm gently moved in and around. I was becoming unglued. He finally brought his fingers out and placed them in his mouth. He then placed his fingers in my mouth. I moaned and he followed with his moans. His hands were on my face and in my hair as we kissed. He had removed his boxers briefs and my thong. I was so impatient at this point that as he grabbed the condom, I reached for it and put it on for him. As he entered me with such force and gentleness at the same time, I gasped as I welcomed him. He was just like I imagined... Exquisite! I was enjoying every inch of him as he took his time with me. My mind was in chaos. The passion that was shared as we made love was so erotic. *How in the world did I get here? I didn't want it to stop*! He was so attentive to my body and made me lose my mind. Malcolm was very experienced. *My god this man!* My hands were holding on to every bicep and muscle I could grip. His hands were rubbing my hair and his lips were on my lips. With his hands in my hair, he moved my head to the side, so he could have my entire neck for his mouth to please. He kept his eyes open as he made love to me. We locked eyes as he continued to make love to me. My body automatically moved in session with him the entire time. Soon after, my body tensed up and released like a sea of crashing waves that couldn't be stopped. I could feel his body tense up as he placed his head into my neck and released a groan that turned me on even more. He released so vigorously and kissed me on my neck, face and mouth. We laid after that and caught our breath. For the longest, we just laid there with no words between us. He grabbed my hand and kissed it. "Alexis," he whispered. I just smiled and closed my eyes. I really didn't know what to say. After a while, we started a conversation. We started with small talk and lots of back and forth compliments. We then talked about our child-hood, our dreams, friends, and jobs. I shared with him how I owned my condo and my car and how I used money that was given to me after my parent's death to purchase both. I was so proud of my current financial situation and savings. I started thinking about my little savings compared to his millions and suddenly felt inadequate again.

Sometime before morning, I was on top of Malcolm. I moaned. He moaned. I kissed. He kissed. As I straddled him, he kept his hands all over me. Malcolm was so good in bed. *Shit.* We continued exploring each other. Everything about him so far was perfect for me. We both collapsed and fell asleep. We woke up to his phones ringing and buzzing off the hook. We were snuggled up with my head on his chest. I got up and went into the bathroom as Malcolm answered his phone. Looking in the mirror, My hair was all over the place but I thought I looked amazing. Sweated our edges and all! Maybe because I felt amazing. I closed my eyes for a second thinking back to our lovemaking. He is addictive. I pray I don't turn into a stalker. I laughed to myself.

Malcolm knocked on the door. "Hey, I have an extra toothbrush for you." He said as he came in. He stopped in his tracks and looked at me real naughty. I was standing there at the sink with nothing but my thong on.

"Thank you," I said. Malcolm walked over to hand me an unopened toothbrush out of his toiletries.

"You are making it hard for me to leave you. Get it?" he said

"I get it," I replied.

I twisted my lips and we both laughed. "I'm trying to figure out how I can leave out this morning without looking like last night and doing the walk of shame." I was thinking about just saying fuck it and getting my proud slutwalk on. Malcolm smiled.

"I wouldn't let you go out like that." "Hold up."

Malcolm left and returned with some of his clothes for me to wear. Riding In the truck on the way back to my condo, I couldn't help but notice how perfect Las Vegas was. The sun was shining and it was already 90 degrees outside. I felt so good.

"If you don't already have plans, Can I cook for you tonight, at my place?" I offered.

"You would cook for me?" he asked with a proud sly smile.

"Yes, I would love to." I replied.

I got out of the truck quickly at my condo. I was wearing a pair of Adidas shorts and an Adidas t-shirt. I even had too big Adidas slip in shoes that Malcolm let me wear. We kissed before we said bye until our dinner date later.

Chapter Eight
Malcolm

The Las Vegas interviews for AMS were relatively easy. Being that we had the prototype in New York already running the music industry, opening up in Vegas was smooth so far. The building was 10 times more upscale than our building in New York. We decided to call the New York site AMS East and the Las Vegas site AMS West. I started the interviews without Drew because he was dealing with an issue with one of our club promoters named Scorpio. We had been in a business with Scorpio for years and brought some of our biggest artists in the industry to his club. He took care of us and the money spent and crowds he had taken care of him and his business. Over time, we've noticed that the club has been going down. The security was not tight enough and the personnel was always changing. Just last week, during a release party for a new rap group to the label, we had to get out quickly for safety. There was a huge fight and guns were being pulled out amongst the guests. The incident was on the news and all over social media. Our label and brand could not risk bad publicity. I flat out told him, we would be looking for another venue if he didn't tighten up his spot. I didn't give him a chance to make it right. We have already set up appearances for a couple of artists at the new club that opens in the city and he's pissed about it.

When Drew returned he updated me on the conversation. He informed me that Scorpio wanted to meet with me and discuss some business. Drew told him that wouldn't probably happen because we all knew Malcolm only moved forward and never backward. Drew said he was cussing and fuming about messing with his money. He ended the call. We got through our interviews and they were successful. We offered and filled at least 10 positions for the West office in Las Vegas. As we waited around the new satellite office, furniture was coming in left and right. My assistant Kim was managing everything in my office and all the receptionist areas. Drew's assistant was taking care of his office and the three board rooms. The AR department was already complete. The new team would oversee the remaining offices and landscaping during the next following weeks. Tebow, Big B, myself and Drew rode back to the hotel together.

The door could barely shut. "So Black who is Lexi?" Drew asked as he looked over his sunglasses at me.

Tebow turned around from the passenger seat as Big B looked straight ahead while driving.

"Lexi is the person I spent last night with." I glared at Tebow who then turned back around to face forward.

"Black! Do you realize I have never seen you smile like that with a female let alone call a female during the middle of the day?" Black was a name that Drew had started calling me back in college.

"I believe it was a FaceTime call, Boss." Tebow corrected.

"So we're doing this today? I asked. "For the record, I just met Lexi. I think she's sexy as hell. She makes me feel a little different. I'm not sure what's going on but I'm enjoying it." *I'm really enjoying it,* I thought to myself. I had a memory of me kissing her open mouth as we made love last night. Lexi was not the typical ass I had been receiving all these years.

"Umm Black! What the hell", I heard. I looked over at Drew who was looking confused.

"I'm good, Drew...just chill" I said as I looked at him then turned my head to look out the window as we pulled up to the hotel.

We got out of the truck. Drew walked up to me and placed his left arm on my right shoulder.

"I'm happy for Evil Knievel plus, happy looks good on your black ass. Are you going out with us tonight?" He asked.

"Naw, I got a hot date." We both laughed.

Heading up to our separate suites we dabbed and agreed to be careful as we enjoyed Vegas for the night. Our plane was leaving at 7am in the morning.

Chapter Nine
ALEXIS

I arrived at my condo a little after 9 am on this beautiful Monday morning. I was very tired but felt like a goddess. I had time to shower and get to work within the next hour or so. I threw on a smoked gray fitted pant suit, a light pink silk camisole and a pair of snakeskin pointed-toe pumps. I ran the flat iron through my hair real quick and threw my oversized sunglasses on. I headed down to the garage to my car. I decided I would drop the top on Sadie, my all black Mercedes coupe this morning. It was a beautiful day in Las Vegas. I was in a great mood as I headed to my office. I turned the music up and sang with Adele, Monica and Nikki. I couldn't help but wonder what Malcolm was doing. I could only hope that he was thinking of me like I was thinking of him. A smile came across my face as I thought about him. The way Malcolm has made me feel in just one day, was hard to explain but gratifying as hell. Damn Stella! Lexi got her groove back!

~

*T*he office was happy to have me back. They had doughnuts and fresh fruit on my conference table in my office. I even had 3 roses in a vase and I knew they were from

Roman. Last year it was 2 roses for each year he has worked with me. My secretary, Maria was the happiest. We even shared a laugh over Roman and those little roses. Bless his heart. Apparently, a few of my casinos had some financial discrepancies and I needed to handle them ASAP. After meeting with Maria for the first hour and signing off on over 50 documents, I cleared out my emails and returned a few phone calls. My calendar for the week was already filling up. Lunch was out of the question today. Maria brought back a tortilla soup from Cafe Rio. Around 1 pm, my phone rang and it was a FaceTime call from Malcolm. I was so happy to see his face. He looked even more handsome. He smiled and I smiled the entire conversation. He told me that the interviews were going good, and he just wanted to see my pretty face. He introduced me to his best friend Drew who was with him. We said hello and talked for a short time. Malcolm then returned to the FaceTime call and I told him I should be home by 6 and was looking forward to having him over for dinner tonight. We both smiled and ended our call.

~

*H*e showed up at 6:30 that evening and was even finer than last night. I greeted him at the door with a kiss. The moans that escaped my mouth and his during the kiss told me how tonight was going down. I got chills thinking about it. I had gotten home about an hour ago and had just enough time to go by the store and shower. I had on a white spaghetti strap sundress that stopped above my knees. My hair was pulled up into a top messy bun, and I was barefoot. I had music playing because I understood that was his world, and we both enjoyed all genres of good music. I also needed something to calm my nerves. Malcolm walked in and loved my condo and the panoramic views of the Las Vegas strip and mountains.

"This Condo is crazy impressive!" He said.

"Thank you."

"How long have you been here?"

"Six years."

"Was it expensive?"

"No. I paid cash when I bought it. This particular unit because it's only 2 bedrooms only cost me $650,000."

"This is great, Baby!" He comfortably said.

I cooked shrimp scampi and whipped up a fresh spinach salad. I poured me a glass of wine.

"Can I get you something to drink?" I asked.

"Water. Please," he replied as he looked around.

"Of course." I smiled.

I already knew this would be my only glass tonight. I was beyond exhausted from the past few days, especially last night and this morning.

Being that the weather was so nice, I decided to set the table out on the patio. Malcolm was in awe of my condo. He continued looking around and walking over to the windows that made up half of the perimeter of my condo. He asked questions about people on my fireplace and I explained who they were and how important they were to me.

At dinner, we talked more in depth about my family and the tragic accident. I explained how I missed them daily. He couldn't understand how I didn't have any family. He asked about a couple of art pieces I had hanging. We laughed and flirted a lot. Our conversation continued to flow so easily. I shared with Malcolm that I ran track in high school, and he shared that he played varsity basketball in high school. In college, neither one of us was athletic and just enjoyed being college students. Malcolm graduated from NYU and I graduated from University Nevada- Las Vegas. We started making references to the night prior.

"I had the best dream last night. Oh, wait. I wasn't dreaming." He said.

"No worries. I had the same dream." I said.

As Malcolm was eating and drinking his lemonade, he said, "this is so good!"

"That sounds familiar," I replied.

We laughed and kept the banter going.

I think we both were anticipating another night like last night.

Malcolm even helped me clean up after dinner. I loved how appreciative and considerate he was to me and always willing to lend a helping hand. Once we were done with the kitchen, I turned off the kitchen lights to get a better view of the strip.

Malcolm came up right behind me and held me for a few minutes as we both admired the breathtaking view for a while.

"I understand now why you like being at home. I would love being here too." We stood wrapped up in each other and looked out over the city. The music was playing, and we just enjoyed being together at that moment.

"Thank you for dinner, Lexi."

"You're welcome. Did you get enough?" I asked.

He turned me around and said, "I don't know if I'll ever get enough."

We kissed and I grabbed his hands and led us to the oversized sofa. He sat down first and I sat on his lap.

"Do you think we will see each other again?" I asked.

"I know we will." He replied.

I looked at him, and we both went in for the kiss. I loved kissing him. We made love once, twice, three times before he left that morning to head back to New York.

Chapter Ten
ALEXIS

*I*t had been 14 days since I last saw Malcolm. We talked nonstop on the telephone using FaceTime. I couldn't even add up the hours we spent on FaceTime each day. He would watch me daily brush my teeth and take a shower. He watched me do my make up, cook dinner and talk to other people at work. He was on the phone when I went to the post office, grocery store, everywhere. I would watch him stare at me and make me feel like the most beautiful woman in the world. I watched and listened as he answered questions and gave out orders all day. I had a chance to learn and listen to the day to day business of a music executive. I often wondered what he was thinking when he looked at me the way he did. We laughed a lot, sent pictures of each other, talked and text nonstop. Even with all the communication we had, I still wanted to touch him. My body craved him. One thing that we both knew about each other was that there was no one of importance in each of our lives. I often heard females flirt with Malcolm while I was on the phone. They were either saying hi or asking if he needed anything. I once heard a female ask if he wanted company and when he turned her down, she continued to make advances. Malcolm was just straight forward. His responses were usually short and consistent with no, thanks, you can leave, peace or now. I noticed that when Malcolm communicated with his assistants, business associates or anyone, he was always serious. It was Friday night and I decided to have drinks with friends from work. I hadn't talked to Malcolm since that morning. He told me he had a big meeting in Manhattan and would call me when he could. That was around 10:00 am.

I headed home around 7:30 pm after my two drinks. I still hadn't heard from him. It had practically been a whole day. I decided to text him to let him know I was headed home. I was feeling a little sad. I hadn't felt like this in a while. I hoped he was okay. This was probably the longest we've not communicated since we met. I called Jess and Eve three-way. I didn't mention anything about not hearing from Malcolm but caught up with their lives. Evelyn was ready to start a family. Unfortunately, her husband Rich was not. Rich already had a daughter and didn't want any more kids just yet. Evelyn was feeling like she was getting the short end of the stick. They had been married for two years now, and she was ready to start having babies. "We have talked and talked, and he just won't budge," Evelyn stated. Her voice was so sad. I was feeling sad for her. Jess on the other hand was very no nonsense and almost militant most of the time. She told Evelyn that she should give him an ultimatum. She added, "What a selfish ass! He knows that you want a baby! I can't believe him and I cannot believe you let him walk over you!" I just suggested marriage counseling. "Evelyn, I feel like y'all owe each other a chance at hearing out how you both feel about starting your family. This could really end badly if y'all don't get counseling." After Evelyn told us he didn't believe in counseling, I somehow eased our conversation to another topic because I was tired and Jess went silent. After about an hour of catching up, we ended our call. I looked at my phone and I still hadn't received a text or call from Malcolm. I didn't know what to think. I prayed that he was okay. I also prayed he wasn't with someone else." I took a hot shower and went to my dresser to pull out some pjs for the night. I saw the t-shirt Malcolm gave me to wear after our first night. I pulled it out to sleep in that night. I went to bed thinking about him. About three hours later I woke up to my phone ringing. I had a FaceTime call. It was Malcolm.

"Hi."

"Hey beautiful," he said.

Through my sleepy eyes, I focused on his eyes that were locked and staring at me.

"What's up. baby? Are you okay?" I asked.

"I really miss you." He said and paused for a while. "I'm sorry I couldn't get away from my business and call you sooner."

"It's okay," I replied.

"I need to be close to you, Lexi."

"I agree. I hate sleeping alone." I added.

I was half coherent but saw that he was taking off his clothes and getting into his bed. I was able to see that beautiful chest and his beautiful tattoos on his entire left shoulder and arm. I soon closed my eyes with that unforgettable sight. I must have fallen asleep because when I woke up the sun was peeking through my door from the living room area. My phone was beside my pillow. The phone had been on this call for 5:44. Five hours and forty-four minutes.

"Malcolm," I called out. "Malcolm," I said again.

"Good morning, beautiful." His deep sleep voice replied.

I was silent.

Seeing him on the screen, my fingers went right to the place I needed him to be. My mind wandered, and I was imagining Malcolm's mouth was where my fingers were currently. I started moaning as I moved my fingers in and out of my wetness. My fingers went in and out with my right hand as my left hand was moving about my breast, mouth and hair. I opened my eyes just enough to see him looking at me with his mouth partly open. I could tell he was turned on. I continued pleasing myself by imagining it was him. My head was twisting and my moans got louder as I sped up my pace of finger penetration. I hit my mission and didn't hold back my moans and sounds.

When I turned back to the screen, Malcolm and I looked at each other. Both our mouths were partly open, but we were not speaking. "I'll see you soon," Malcolm said and hung up. I knew I had to see him. Phone sex just made things worse. It was fun and my first experience and although I climaxed for him, I craved him even more. I was a mess. Malcolm called back about 30 minutes later and said he would be in Vegas by 4:30 pm that evening. I had five hours to get ready and pick him up at Las Vegas McCarran Executive Terminal.

Chapter Eleven

ALEXIS

*P*ulling into the private terminal was scary. I was actually on the same terminal as the private jets. No, soon I pulled in, Malcolm was calling me. I answered and he said keep coming to the right. His plane was the white with navy stripes and huge AMS letters on it. Malcolm looked amazing! He exited the private plane wearing cargo shorts and a designer black polo shirt and a pair of black sneakers. I opted for a sleeveless emerald green sundress. One shoulder strap stayed up and the other was off the shoulder. I wore a pair of flesh tone dainty 4-inch sandals.

It was a windy August afternoon but it was at least 110 degrees outside. I didn't care that my hair was blowing all over. I was just happy to feel Malcolm in my arms again. He held me so tight as we kissed.

"I missed you," I said.

"I missed you more, beautiful. I can't kiss you too much here because I'm one second from taking you right here outside!" He said as he looked me in my eyes. His eyes had "that" look and I knew that look well now.

We stopped on our way back to my place for lunch. We had lunch at Maggiano's Italian restaurant. Malcolm and I sat, smiled and ate lunch like we were the only two people on earth. We couldn't keep our hands and mouths off each other. We had no idea that pictures were being snapped. We walked through the shops. Malcolm wanted to stop by to see a jeweler he knew.

We went in and I came out with a pair of diamond earrings that I know cost too much. "Happy Belated Birthday, baby!" Malcolm said.

"My birthday was in May." I looked puzzled.

He insisted I accept them and said it was my birthday gift that he never gave me. I decided to just say thank you and keep it moving. Several people had recognized him by now. They were very respectful and just spoke as we walked past them hand in hand. It was Saturday, and he had to be back by Monday morning. That night me and Malcom didn't come up for air. I convinced him to play truth or dare, and he introduced a game called never have I ever...and let me be clear...everything I have now. Malcolm was not afraid of anything and made me feel so free and sexy. I loved exploring with him.

That Sunday, we went swimming in the pool at the condo. It was hot in Vegas! I packed us a bag full of snacks, water, fruit and pool essentials. I even brought my small Bluetooth for music. I wore a red two-piece bikini. Malcolm had on a pair of black trunks.

"Is that what you're wearing to the pool?" he asked.

"Yes. Is something wrong with it?"

"Is this a public pool?" he looked confused.

"Yes. What's wrong with my swimsuit?"

I started trying to adjust my straps and shit.

"Nothing is wrong with your swimsuit. You look freaking stunning! Baby, I might be selfish because I don't want anyone enjoying the view of you." He started getting that look. He moved in on me with his hands on my hips. "You keep me wanting you. This red looks sexy as hell on you. All I'm saying is I don't want any problems."

I kissed him.

"Thank you. I promise we won't have any problems." I smiled.

The pool was more like a resort. It was complete with three massive waterfalls and two tunnels. One had a swim up bar. We found an area, put our stuff on two lounge chairs and dived into the pool. The water felt magical! We swam across the pool and came up laughing. My hair was all over the place, so I just slid my ponytail holder off my wrist and on my hair to a high bun on top of my head. We swam back over towards our chairs and came up again.

"I'm having so much fun," I whispered as my lips touched his.

"Me too." Malcolm's eyes made my heart and insides go crazy.

We kissed and made out at the pool on this perfect Sunday. He carried me through the water on his back. We spent the entire after-noon at the pool. At one point while I was lying on the lounge chair, as the sun was setting, I looked up just as Malcolm was coming out of the pool. Everything seemed to be in slow motion. His normal dark complexion was even darker and his wet body reminded me of an expensive piece of artwork! Watching him walk toward me, damn near made me have an orgasm. Malcolm was drying off and sat next to me.

"You okay? He asked.

I quickly said, "I'm good." I went in for a quick kiss. Malcolm leaned in and placed one hand on my cheek. He started moving his thumb down my face to my lips and kissed me again. This time the kiss was a lot more passionate.

"I like your hair curly." He said as he played with my hair.

I smiled. "Thank you! I really like you!"

He did the crooked sly smile with his lips together and shook his head up and down. That night, I experienced the best shower sex ever. It started with my legs wrapped around his waist and my back up against the shower wall. I ended with my hands against the wall after Malcolm had me turn around and bend over. The climax I experienced for the first time this way had me calling god and cursing interchangeably.

Monday morning came quickly. Malcolm and I were already planning our next visit. Malcolm had invited me to a party at his home in New York. I said I couldn't make it because it was on a

Thursday night and I had to work. The party was 10 days away. I purchased my round trip ticket. I told Malcolm I would probably come to see him that Friday, but I was coming in on Thursday to surprise him at the party he was hosting for some artists on his label. I was so excited, I could hardly wait.

Chapter Twelve
Jess

We were on our typical three-way FaceTime call.

"What if he's with another bitch?" I asked.

"Really Jess? Why do you always have to be so fucking negative?" Lexi asked.

"I'm not being negative, I'm being realistic." I defended myself.

"No bitch you're being negative!" Evelyn, who was visibly upset, added,

"You just don't stop, Jess! Lexi doesn't do shit nor have a life and when she finally starts living, here your militant ass comes with that typical Debbie the downer shit!" Evelyn shouted.

"Debbie the downer? You know what? Fuck you, Evelyn!" I shouted back.

"You know what... I'm grown and don't need no one's approval or opinion! Bye bitches!"Lexi hung up.

After that, we all hung up.

I poured me a glass of Stella Rosa. I couldn't believe they made me the bad guy, again! I love Lexi and Evelyn but I'm tired of both of them and their bad decisions with men. Lexi was the smartest and prettiest girl I knew in college. When she walked into a room everyone took notice. She was stunning, to say the least. Lexi has that brown sugar complexion and long black hair. Her eyes were soft, yet exotic with her full eyelashes. Lexi's beautiful smile and perfect lips could gain the attention of any man. My best friend also had that amazing body. She had a small waist and thick thighs. There has never been an outfit Alexis Bell couldn't rock and look flawless in. She graduated with honors from college despite the great loss she suffered. The spring Lexi lost her entire family in a car accident, Evelyn flew back home with her and my family was there in a matter of days. My mom, dad and grandparents flew to Vegas with me to be there for her during the memorial services. Lexi couldn't speak for days. The doctor put her on anti-depressants. After the funeral, Evelyn and I stayed with her for the summer. She was so depressed and cried daily for months. My mom helped her with all the financial affairs and the funeral. That summer, Lexi went through a lot and had a hard time getting past her loss. She lost so much weight where we were all scared. She was in therapy twice a week, and we made sure she went. That fall, Lexi wanted to return to school, and she did. Returning to school helped her with her depression. Three years later, we all graduated. Lexi graduated from a different college. We were very protective of her. I'm still protective of her. I liked this new guy Malcolm but his world was completely different from hers. He had the potential to hurt her really bad. I have been hearing about him since she met him. Lexi is falling for this man and I don't know if he feels the same.

My phone rang.

"Hello."

"Hey," Evelyn said. "I'm sorry things got out of hand. I just need you to try to let Lexi be happy." "When was the last time we saw her this happy and living outside her condo?"

"You're right. She is happy." I admitted. "Evelyn, I just don't want her to be hurt and go through another depression. I'm worried about her." I took another sip of my wine. "If this Malcolm dude breaks her heart, I'm going to kill the son of a bitch!" I stated.

"We know, bitch! He just might be what's good for her." Evelyn said with hope in her voice.

Let's call this slut! I said, and we both laughed as we called her back on the three-way Facetime.

Chapter Thirteen
ALEXIS

My flight arrived Thursday evening at exactly 7:00. I changed at the airport and hopped in an Uber straight to his house. I wore a beautiful black strapless tulle bottom dress. I wore an exquisite pair of black crystal Christian Louboutins. Pulling up to his stunning mansion, I panicked. His house was not a house but a fucking castle. What was I doing? Jess' words ran through my mind...*"What if you surprise him, and he has another bitch there with him?"* I had quickly decided that if he was indeed occupied with someone else, I would just leave. There was a greeter at the door who let me place my bag in a front closet. I was grateful because a few people were looking at me strangely as I rolled up the walkway, dressed to the nines, with a suitcase. I was floored at how huge and beautiful his home was. It reminded me of a museum. This house was really massive. Mansion in every sense of the word. People were wall to wall everywhere! My stomach was flipping out from being so nervous. I hoped I hadn't made a mistake. I made my way through the crowded rooms. There were way more women than men. Every female in here was beautiful! I also noticed that *sexy* was the attire. The women here either had on minimal clothing, big boobs or huge asses. Some had all three. A few females blatantly gave me the "oh hell no" look as I walked past. I didn't know them but apparently, they acted like they knew me. The music was extra loud but was banging. If I wasn't so nervous, I would have already grabbed a glass off one of the trays being carried around by the servers and on the dance floor. I scanned the rooms as I continued to walk through until I spotted my Malcolm. There he was in the back of the main room standing talking with his friend Drew and three females. His back was to me but I knew that was him. He was in a black tailored suit and white dress shirt. He looked so perfect. Seeing him here in this setting made him look distinguished. He looked like he belonged here and this was his world.

Malcolm turned around as if he knew I was there. As soon as our eyes connected my heart started beating so fast. I was praying he was not upset with me for surprising him. Now all of a sudden, I felt foolish for not giving him a heads up about my plans. Malcolm came directly toward me. It seemed like everyone followed him with their eyes and immediately focused on us.

Without hesitation, Malcolm's hands went to my face and his lips on my lips. It was a short kiss followed by "When did you get to New York and how did you get here?"

I was still in his embrace and looked around at the multiple eyes indiscreetly looking at us. He turned my face back so that my eyes were looking directly at him.

"I wanted to surprise you," I whispered.

I was starting to second guess my decision to surprise him. I was staring directly in his eyes and could feel my tears getting ready to fall.

Malcolm looked puzzled and placed his forehead on my forehead and whispered back, "I'm so happy you're here. I was missing you like crazy. This is the best surprise!"

"By the way," he paused.

"You look good enough to eat and I'm starving." He said as he stared at me.

The smile that stretched across my face, was followed by a slight giggle.

Malcolm then grabbed my hands and took me over to where he was standing when I walked in. He formally introduced me to Drew, his partner in crime and a female that was with him named Carla. Drew hugged me like we knew each other. It made me feel good. He was about an inch shorter than Malcolm. Drew had a bad boy look about him with his long eyelashes, but he was very handsome. His complexion was more of an olive tone and his hair was thick and black. Drew wore his hair a little longer on the top of his fade compared to Malcolm who kept his hair short on his fade. They both had the same facial mustache and beard. Drew was almost identical to Malcolm in size and style. I could see why they were best friends. I could also see how the two of them could get into a lot of trouble. The other two ladies walked off as we walked up. I saw the side eye roll before they left. Carla was very genuine and smiled at me. We stood and made small talk with the two of them for a while.

Malcolm took the time to walk me throughout most of the party and introduce me to people he worked with, I met his assistant, Kim, members of his security detail, and many other people. He may have only introduced me as Lexi to everyone, but the way his hands never left mine, told them all otherwise. The women seemed to be whispering, watching and giving faces but I honestly didn't care. I felt good and was extremely happy to be here. I even threw a little extra sass in my walk because I felt good and knew I looked good!

After hours of walking around inside and out, I stood by the DJ Platform while Malcolm circulated throughout the party. The DJ had everyone moving. I saw Drew and Carla dancing and having a great time. I had a feeling that she and I would become better acquainted through the guys. There were female dancers in every area of the property dancing on huge blocks. It felt like I was in an upscale club. I had a drink in one hand and my clutch in the other. The DJ played *You the Boss* by Rick Ross and my hips did a little extra swaying as I sang *I'll do anything that you say anything cause you the Boss.* As soon as I looked up, I saw Malcolm looking at me from across the room. I kept singing as he headed straight towards me. You the boss... aye. As soon as he reached me, Malcolm placed his hands on my hips and whispered in my ear "come dance with me."

I put my drink and clutch on the DJ table and with my hand, in his, we stepped on the dance floor. I noticed that everyone seemed to have stopped and started watching us. It was a strange feeling. I heard someone yell, "aw shit! Go, X!" He looked extremely sexy, happy and gorgeous. Pelvic to Pelvic, I did what felt right. Malcolm was a great dancer. He danced so close to me and made me feel sexy as hell. I danced seductively and sang every word to him as I stayed in sync with him. Before I knew it I turned my back to him and had gone to the floor and back up. He put his arms around me from the back, and we continue to move. I closed my eyes and enjoyed being in his embrace. I loved dancing with Malcolm. Dancing with him was such a turn on. He matched every move I made and was almost showing me up. I was impressed. I could feel him and I knew he could feel me.

After the song went off Malcolm received all kinds of dabs and high fives. His friends were all talking shit because they said they had never seen him dance. He wasn't saying much but was just smiling. I went to stand by the DJ booth again. Malcolm came over to me.

"Are you about ready to lay down?" he asked in my ear.

With one eyebrow up and a huge smile across my face, I answered him with a question.

"Are you ready to lay me down?" He made a grunting noise, kissed me on my cheek and said he will be right back.

As soon as Malcolm walked off, four females came and stood about six feet from where I was standing. All of them looked like low budget strippers! I already knew they were coming with the shit. I sipped my drink and stood there.

I heard one of them say, "someone thought this was a prom."

Another one talked about how she knows this house like the back of her hand. Her friends were laughing and agreeing, as one of them said, "you definitely know X's bed." They were saying a lot of bullshit to piss me off.

I then heard "I know what he is working with and I know what he likes and that ain't it!"

They laughed and headed towards me.

Never taking my eyes off these bitches, I placed my drink down.

They walked past me and went outside to the pool area. I contemplated leaving. I knew I could never really have a future with Malcolm. My father always told me to choose who and what I let waste my time because time was something you couldn't get back. I had already wasted too much time in my past relationships.

As I was walking towards the front door, I saw Malcolm walking towards me with Drew. With a look of concern, Malcolm asked "Where are you going, baby?" As soon as he spoke and I looked at his eyes, I felt it. I knew I could trust him and I knew that he hadn't done anything to me. I wanted to tell him about what had just happened, but couldn't. I just shook my head to say I was going *nowhere*. He whispered something in Drew's ear. Malcolm grabbed my hand, and we headed toward the back of the stairwell in his home. It was after 1:00 am and the party was still in full swing. We stood in front of a small elevator and Malcolm placed my hand on a screen, and he then pushed some buttons. He asked me to place my hand back on the screen and the doors open immediately. He hurried me in and the doors shut quick and hard. He explained to me that this was a secret shortcut that I could use if I ever had to go up and down from the master bedroom. He also warned me that the doors closed within 2 seconds of sensing you crossing into the elevator and to be careful. Malcolm then stood in front of me and kissed me with such force, that his strength pushed me against the elevator wall. We were gearing up when the elevator opened up on the second floor. We stepped out into a small room with over 25 screens and camera footage of the property outside and multiple common area rooms. We then went through another solid door and stepped into the largest bedroom I had ever been in. It was dark and full of solid dark wood furniture. His colors were dark red and accents of cream and gold. This room should be featured in a movie or magazine. I was definitely impressed. The room was facing the back of the property and the view out of his windows was of the yard and pool. I could look out and down and view the party that was still going on. Malcolm's yard was amazingly beautiful and looked like it was made for entertaining. I turned around and looked at Malcolm who was watching me. I walked over to him. He had a very focused and serious look on his face.

"What are you thinking?" I asked.

He answered immediately with a deep tone.

"I'm thinking about how happy I am that you're here tonight. I'm also thinking how happy I would be if you said you could stay for a couple of weeks."

I smiled some more and said "What would you do with me for weeks, Malcolm? You don't think you would get tired of me?"

Malcolm removed his jacket and unbuttoned one of his buttons on his shirt. "I don't think I could ever get tired of you." I just watched his lips as they were already within an inch of mine. "I need to know, are you mine?"

"Am I yours?" I asked. "I'm confused."

"Are you mine? I want you to be and I need you to be, Lexi." Malcolm grabbed me around my waist and pulled me into him and I felt his arousal. We began kissing and I felt like I had been hypnotized. I quietly responded, "I want to be yours."

Malcolm kissed me and let out a deep groan. We kissed until I was sitting on his huge bed. Malcolm got down on his knees and started running his fingers down my face, neck and arms. I closed my eyes and enjoyed his touch. He then went under my dress with his face. Malcolm had my thighs locked with his arms. He was not giving me any room to move. I was squirming and grabbing the bedding. I was losing control quickly. "Malcolm," I cried out. "Malcolm, oh shit!" I shouted as my head fell back. My stomach muscles felt like they would be bruised and my body was going through convulsions. He didn't let up and I released like clockwork. The intimacy Malcolm and I shared that night as we made love was the point of no return for both of us. Everything I needed to know was spoken to me by the way he made love to me that night.

"I love you," I whispered as I was dozing off.

Chapter Fourteen

ALEXIS

That morning we woke up late, took a shower together and headed down to the kitchen. The house was so clean like there was never a party. Malcolm gave me a tour of the house. His home could be described as immaculate. The kitchen was spectacular. Malcolm and I could not keep our hands off each other as we laughed about nothing. I snuggled up under him as much as I could. My happy place had quickly turned into Malcolm. No matter how close I was to him physically, I wanted to be even closer. We kissed and hugged around the large kitchen counter. Malcolm made us a great breakfast. Between kisses, we feed each other. We even drank our juice out of the same glass. The emptiness I had once felt was long gone. Malcolm said he had plans for us today. We headed back upstairs and got dressed. I wore a pair of black satin parachute pants and a black halter top. I completed my outfit with a pair of 3 inch cheetah strap sandals. I flat ironed my hair and threw on my sunglasses. Malcolm had on jeans and a white silk T-shirt. He threw his sunglasses on too.

Malcolm and I headed to Manhattan and enjoyed a quick bite at this quaint sushi restaurant. So many people came up to Malcolm and even more, snapped pictures of him and us as we left the restaurant and got back into his blacked out Lamborghini Huracan.

We then drove to an upscale mall. When we pulled into valet, Malcolm took hold of my hand and told me to just keep walking and try to act like I don't even see them. As soon as we stepped into the store, we were escorted to the back area. Malcolm sat on a plush couch while they measured me. After that clothes were being brought back by the dozens. I couldn't even pronounce half of the things Malcolm had me try on. I do know that everything I picked out would be delivered to the house today. I found out that Malcolm added scarfs, coats and more clothes that he wanted me to have that I didn't even try on. He also had them pick out designer purses, perfumes, underwear, intimate apparel, shoes, and jewelry.

We drove about an hour out of the city limits. The entire ride was such fun. We held and kissed each other's hands, talked and sang with the music playing. Gotta Be by Jagged Edge was playing, and we sang the song like we wrote it. We pulled up at a cemetery. We went to his mom's gravesite.

"I hope you're okay with coming here?" he asked.

"Of course I am," I replied. We walked toward a massive headstone. Malcolm introduced me to his mom. He talked to her as if we were standing in her home, and she was alive. He knelt down close to her grand headstone and told his mom that he missed her. He told her that he met someone, but he was sure that she already knew. He told her that he needed her to continue to look after him. He then asked if she would look after us. He asked her to continue to guide him. He also told her that she would be seeing me again. "I'm in love, mom." and I was one day going to be his wife. He asked if I had anything to say. I was so shocked at what I had just heard that I hadn't realized I had a tear rolling down my face. I wiped my tears and knelt down beside Malcolm. I was familiar with visits to a cemetery because I visited my family often. Malcolm grabbed my hand. I said hello and thanked his mom for such an amazing son. I told her my name and that I wished I had met her in person. I also told her that Malcolm was one of a kind. I told her that I loved how special their relationship was and that I was looking forward to coming to visit her again.

"Thank you for Malcolm," I smiled. I promised her I would never leave him and would take care of him.

That night Malcolm and I just laid and watched movies. He played in my hair. I laid on his lap. We talked and enjoyed our time. That night while making love he told me that he loves me.

That Saturday, we had dinner with his closest friends mostly from the AMS. The dinner consisted of at least 30 people. The guests consisted of mostly couples. Malcolm looked so happy. Drew stood up to make a toast. Everyone held their glasses up. "This toast is to friends that are more like family. A special toast to my brother Malcolm and his beautiful girl, Lexi. Thank you, Lexi, for coming into X's life and making him the happiest any of us has ever seen him!" Everyone cheered and drank. "Thank you", Malcolm said. He even took a sip of champagne after the toast. Everyone clapped and made jokes about him being "smitten" and falling "in love" and said things like, "it's about time." I was confused. What was Malcolm really like before me? I just kissed him and talked with whoever talked with me that night. I mostly spent my time with Carla drinking as she gave me the tea on everyone there. It was a great evening.

Chapter Fifteen
Drew

"I believe Lexi is the one. I took her to the gravesite this morning." Malcolm said. I'm shocked but not shocked. Malcolm had been my best friend for years. We knew everything about each other and I knew early on that Lexi was someone important.

"Black! I'm speechless! I'm happy for both of you. I also think she is perfect for you and I approve!" We both laughed.

Laughing was something X hardly did. It felt good to see this side of him. I crack jokes all day and would get a smirk and maybe a head shake saying "you a fool, man" from him. Since he's met Lexi Bell, my brother has been outright laughing, smiling, cheesing, whatever you want to call it. In the last month, he has danced, talked on the phone, and only been with her. He talks about her and looks at her like he's sometimes like he's in disbelief that she's real. Lexi was very pretty and had a way about herself. Her personality was the opposite of his, and she didn't bite her tongue. She was definitely the one for him! Malcolm did tell me that he was worried about his past catching up with him. He said if Lexi ever knew the details of his past, he worried she would bow out gracefully. He told me two weeks ago that he didn't want to label groupies around him, and he gave me his other phone and asked me to hide it for him. He told the whole team that he wasn't interested or available for any female other than Lexi. He even shared with me that he felt between God and his mom that they led him to her because he very rarely or never flew commercial flights. That day was rare and out of his norm. That day was meant to happen. For over 10 years, Malcolm has been the most serious person I know. As Co-CEO of AMS music, he was and has always deemed the most respected and consistent brother in the business. His motto was, *You're only as good as your word.* Because of this, we were able to sign and work with many artists. He had created a lot of millionaires. He's never had a serious relationship or dated anyone exclusively but always had women that he dealt with to fulfill his needs. Malcolm was known for not giving affection or letting females spend the night with him. I can remember someone accused him of being an "undercover brother" because he was so secretive. When that rumor came out, I just knew he was going to lose his mind. He didn't let it bother him the least bit. The rumor has never circulated again. Now when you see him, he's constantly kissing Lexi, and they practically live together every chance they get. Malcolm and Lexi were all over social media. Their couple's name was *XLex* on social media and every picture displayed their admiration of each other.

"Do you need me to bring anything for dinner?" I asked.

"Naw. I'm just looking forward to introducing Lexi to my team." Malcolm said.

"Bet! Also, moms said she called you three days ago and you haven't called her back yet. You know she can't go longer than 4 days without talking to her beloved Malcolm!" I said.

"I'm calling her now!" He replied. We said our goodbyes and ended the call.

My parents loved Malcolm. My mom always asked me why I couldn't be more like him? If only she knew! I laughed to myself. Tonight we were having a dinner party at Malcolm's house. He was excited about introducing Lexi to everyone. I decided to call Carla to see if she wanted to go with me. I already knew the answer. I met Carla a couple of years ago at the grand opening of her third beauty bar and spa. I liked her a lot but I knew she wasn't the one.

Carla was successful, sweet and pretty, but she lacked the ambition or grit I like in women. I would love to see her tough side sometimes. Carla has tried to get me to commit to her on several occasions but as soon as she doesn't hear what she wants, she ends up crying and eventually leaving for a few days. My mom and dad liked her, so I kept the relationship going. Maybe one day I will eventually fall in love with her and have a romance like my brother and Lexi?

Chapter Sixteen
ALEXIS

That night we went out to one of the clubs he frequents whenever he has an artist in town or whenever he's entertainment industry friends. I had never been with an entourage but this night we traveled with damn near 50 people! Malcolm and I rode with Drew, Tebow and Big B in one truck. Drew even had a date with him. It wasn't Carla. Once we entered the club, we were escorted up some stairs to the VIP area. Malcolm and Drew were like celebrities! They dabbed and said hello to so many people, it took us forty-five minutes to get to sit. I sat close to Malcolm because there was a lot of shit going on. The music was loud and everyone was drinking and dancing. In our area alone, bitches were on these dudes like white on rice. They were lap dancing and taking bottles to the head. I had to adjust my face. Malcolm gave me a peck on the cheek. I wore a little black silk dress with the entire back out tonight. The back was so low and was accented with three silver chains at my butt crack. Not to mention it stopped mid thigh. This was one of the pieces Malcolm picked out. I complimented my little black dress with a pair of Gucci chain heels. Malcolm had a hairstylist come over, and she washed and flat ironed my hair with the part down the middle. I was feeling very sexy. Malcolm tried everything he could to get me before we left the house. I wasn't getting set up!

We decided to stand up in a cozy little corner because if one more female approached me or Malcolm, I was going to check a bitch. With him in the corner and me in front of him dancing, I knew no one would approach us. My back was to Malcolm but my body was against him as I swayed to the music.

"You know we are not going to be here long," he whispered in my ear.

"Why not?" I asked. I could actually feel why.

"For one, You look too damn fine for me not to be feasting on you right now. Two, you're leaving me tomorrow. Three, I'm selfish and need you all to myself right now." I turned my head to look at him, and he threw the look on me with those sexy eyes. My insides jumped immediately. I leaned in his ear "I'm ready right now, baby

Before I could finish, Malcolm pushed me away from him and grabbed my hand. "Let's go," he muttered. He was dabbing and saying bye to his boys when I felt something strange and uncomfortable in my spirit. I looked over and some guy was looking me up and down as he came towards us.

"What's up playboy?" he said to Malcolm and reached out to greet him.

Malcolm went in for his usual dab with this creepy dude. I noticed the creepy guy had a couple of guys like security guards with him.

"You aren't leaving X are you?" he asked.

"Yeah, We're heading out. This is my girl Lexi. Lexi this is Scorpio, he owns this club and is one of our business partners."

"Should be your only business partner," Scorpio said, sucking his teeth.

"Hi, nice to meet you" as I held my hand out to shake his hand.

Scorpio took my hand and placed it on his lips. *Fix your face, Lexi.* I knew my face was twisted and fucked up. I instantly felt Malcolm tense up while holding my left hand. As Scorpio sucked his teeth and looked me up and down, he rubbed on his penis and said, "you def not from around here brown sugar. If you were, I would have snatched your pretty ass off the street quick..." I'm not sure what happened exactly after that because everything went so fast. Malcolm was in his face like a pit bull in a dog fight. His security team was one step ahead of him. Scorpio boys were on it too. Drew was holding Malcolm back and everyone held their hand on their piece. "You ever come at me or mine like that again, you will regret it motherfucker" Malcolm said with his mouth barely moving and as serious as I have ever seen him. He grabbed my hand, and we were escorted out with some guys from Malcolm's security detail. I heard Scorpio yell something like, "payback is a bitch!" As we were walking down from VIP and out of the club.

People had their phones out and recorded the whole incident. Once we were in the truck at least four SUVs rolled out. We were in the second one. The music was so loud in the truck. I was feeling anxious and Malcolm was quiet while holding my hand.

"I'm sorry baby. I'm sorry that you had to be a part of this bull-shit. I will never allow anyone to disrespect you or me," Malcolm said.

"I understand," I replied as I leaned into his chest on our ride back to the house.

"You know I can fight, right?" I said.

Malcolm did his smirk, "I bet you can."

He turned toward me and placed one hand on my exposed thigh and hip with the other hand he lifted my chin and kissed my lips. He moved his hand to the back of my head, and we kissed all the way home. We made love all night. We could never seem to get enough of each other. I can honestly say, I can be with him all day and every day and never get enough. Saying bye was getting harder and harder.

Chapter Seventeen

Malcolm

I had a bad feeling. Last night was the first time I actually had a run in with him. Scorpio was a bad guy who turned clean and over the last couple of years reverted back to his old ways of being a bad guy. Everyone in the community knew his story. Scorpio was bad news. For the last year, we've had a few misunderstandings. The streets talk loud in New York and I had heard enough lately to know we needed to unaffiliate ourselves from him and his club. AMS Music could no longer promote our artists through his club. The streets informed me of all the shit he was doing illegally. I had heard everything from dealing with drugs to sex trafficking through his night club. Scorpio knew I was the one who gave the directive that AMS was done with him. Nothing could get me back in his janky ass club or with his hating ass crew. I also found out after the fact, that I apparently had sex with his girlfriend. Let the streets tell it, she was *"The one female he truly loved."* I remember the female but I didn't know she was involved with Scorpio. I remember the yacht party and I remember doing her and her friend on the upper deck of the yacht. There is no way I would have disrespected Scorpio like that had I known that was *his* girl. I also knew last night was personal.

Chapter Eighteen

ALEXIS

That Sunday evening I returned to Vegas. He was adamant about me traveling in first class and paid for the upgrade. He even tried to buy out the seat next to me but I said, "absolutely not." That week we went back to our jobs and talked on the phone all day, every day. I buried myself in work to stay busy. I had started being recognized when I was out. I just spoke back and kept moving.

By that Friday Malcolm was in Vegas with me for the weekend. We just enjoyed each other in every way. We spent days and nights making love to each other. I would dance around the house all the time for him, and he loved it. We went out shopping and ate at the best restaurants. Malcolm knew so many people and everyone seemed to know him. He made appearances at a few clubs and I danced every chance I got. We made love so much. I cannot explain it. We craved each other more and more. It's like the more we made love the more love making we wanted. I was used to being in the gossip blogs and social media by now. Jess shared links to articles and forwarded pictures every chance she could. I still refused to do social media. At first, I was the mystery woman with X Styles from our first weekend out. Then I was called his girlfriend. There were pictures of me getting in the truck on our first night. Pictures of us at the pool kissing and laying on the lounge chairs. They had pictures from the party at his house, our dinners, and of course the crazy night at the club. In one article they had quotes from sources in his circle stating that he had changed and was predicting wedding bells soon. Malcolm didn't care. I didn't care either. He kissed me anywhere and all the time and I loved it. We had started signing our text messages to each other. TeamXLex!

Chapter Nineteen

ALEXIS

*E*very weekend for the next three months, we were together. I went back to NY for a few weekends. Each trip to New York was better than the previous one. I was really loving the east coast, especially Manhattan. On one of our dinner dates, at an upscale restaurant in Manhattan, we ran into Scorpio. As he was leaving the restaurant, we were sitting down to eat. He and his disgusting goons started laughing as they looked at us. Scorpio had a shit face grin that made me sick to my stomach. Malcolm tried to tell me to ignore them but it was too late! I had already thrown the middle finger up! The exchange the guys gave each other was not good and the stank face I gave Scorpio was worse. No words were spoken but I hated the queasy feeling in the pit of my stomach. As soon as we sat down Malcolm sent a few texts, and we enjoyed our dinner. I finally asked him what was the beef between him and Scorpio? Malcolm explained everything to include the girls on the yacht last summer. I would be lying if I say I wasn't upset about the girls but the reality of it was that I was not even in his life back then. Also, while eating dinner, Malcolm informed me that in two weeks, he was taking me on a vacation. I soon forgot about the Scorpio drama and was looking forward to this baecation with Malcolm. We flew out of Vegas on the private jet to Mexico. The four-day getaway to Cabo was one for the books! Malcolm and I went to a tattoo artist on the island. I got a half sleeve tattoo on my right fore-arm. I opted for three huge red roses with green and black leaves throughout. The word LOVE was integrated throughout. Malcolm had the same thing on his right forearm but with black ink only to match his others. This was my first tattoo and I loved doing it with Malcolm. We had the best time.

Now that the weather was changing to fall, Malcolm preferred Vegas to NY. Malcolm's house in Vegas was finally ready. The closing was just like they promised the end of October. His home was beyond massive and beautiful. It was located in a guard gated community and behind another set of private gates. He paid 5.7 million for this beauty. He had given me the carte blanche on every-thing in his home. I worked with his Realtor and a team of decora-tors and contractors daily for the last two months. I made sure he would be happy, and he was!

Chapter Twenty
Scorpio

Scorpio had received his name from the streets. When he was 15 years old while sleeping in his uncle's basement, he was bitten by a scorpion on his left cheek. His uncle didn't believe in going to any medical facilities and decided to treat it himself. That home remedy treatment left a scar on his face and that's how the neighborhood came up with the name Scorpio for him. That same year, Scorpio was arrested for selling drugs to an undercover cop on the streets. He would eventually spend the next 10 years in and out of the judicial system from charges of drug possession, probation violation and even assault and battery. A couple of years after his release from prison, at the age of 27 years old, Scorpio's uncle passed away. His uncle left him a little money through a life insurance policy. Scorpio, now having a pregnant girlfriend, wanted to go legit. He was in love with Tammy, who was a gold digger to the core. Getting money from men by shaking her ass was her livelihood. She was a stripper at one of the strip clubs in the city. Within one month of dating Scorpio, she told him she was pregnant. He moved her into his home and planned on marrying her. That was never her plan. She told him she miscarried their baby and against his wishes, she quickly resorted back to her trifling lifestyle. Her days and nights consisted of stripping, partying, smoking blunts and sleeping around. Scorpio bought his club and poured everything into the club. He became very successful. Over the last six years, he and Tammy have been in several fights. She always left but came right back when she needed a place to live. In the last year, Scorpio had quickly turned back to his old ways.

~

*P*ayback is a bitch and X will get his. First, you fucked with my money then you fucked my bitch! Scorpio was sitting in his half lit office at his desk talking to himself. He had been thinking about how he would deal with Malcolm and the disrespect he was feeling. A smile came across his face as he heard in his head... *an eye for an eye: a tooth for a tooth and a bitch for a bitch!* Scorpio had his plan, and he knew this would destroy X. He picked up his phone as he got excited just thinking about it. His plan included recording it for everyone to see. *That pretty little bitch is going to get exactly what she asked for at the restaurant.*

Chapter Twenty-One

ALEXIS

"Wow, Baby," he exclaimed! "What in the world! This is perfect! I love every room and all the elaborate touches put into the details." He walked around this 14,000 square foot home in absolute Awe. Every room was fully furnished. The new home had 8 bedrooms and 10 bathrooms. A state-of-the-art white gourmet kitchen. A music studio, white Italian marble floors throughout the entire house, a gym, tennis courts, movie room, infinity pool and a to-die-for swivel grand staircase. The master suite was one out of a magazine. The master suite was larger than my condo. The sitting area and spa bathroom were on a drop level compared to the bed that sat up on a pedestal with a custom wall panel 8-foot headboard that went from the floor to the ceiling. The entire room was white with glass walls. The retractable screens and boutique-store-style closet was the icing on the cake. Malcolm was beside himself.

"I have no words, Baby!" Malcolm said as he placed his forehead on mine, closed his eyes and began kissing me. I opened my mouth to welcome his strong tongue and moaned as we stood there and communicated with our mouths.

That night Malcolm had a team come out and set up an outdoor dinner for two. With the weather being 79 degrees and the beautiful oasis backyard, the set up was remarkable. To my surprise, Malcolm had a custom closet full of a complete wardrobe set up for me in this house. I was close to tears thinking about the ways he goes over and beyond for me. It made me feel so special; I was getting used to being spoiled by him. After dinner, Malcolm wanted to walk around the perimeter of the property. As we turned towards the east of the property, there was a complete rose garden with a sitting area and walking trail. I stopped in my tracks. One tear fell and then the next. This was the most beautiful rose garden I had ever seen.

We spent the rest of the week together in the new house. He didn't go back to New York yet and wasn't even entertaining the thought of me not staying there with him. During that week, I went to my condo during my lunch break to check my mail and let some fresh air in. My condo looked like a closet compared to the mansion I had been living in this past week with Malcolm. This upcoming Saturday, Malcolm was my date to a fundraiser gala. I told him he didn't have to go, but he insisted. The ball was inside of a casino in one of the grand ballrooms. He looked so handsome in his tux. I opted for a long black strap gown with off the shoulder straps and crystals throughout. I paired them with a pair of blinged out heels.

Chapter Twenty-Two

ALEXIS

*A*s soon as we walked in, eyes turned in our direction. A couple of hostesses recognized me because I was an award recipient. I was being recognized for my continued contribution and community service to the local community college where my father was tenured. Yet, the attention we were getting was mostly because people recognized Malcolm immediately. We were escorted to our table which was reserved for the honorees. The ballroom was gorgeous. Before we could sit down a couple came over and introduced themselves. From there several others came over and took pictures with us. Everyone was very nice.

"Hi, Lexi Lou!"

As soon as I heard the voice, I closed my eyes. It was my ex, Sean. I turned around.

"Hi, How are you?" I responded not really caring but trying to be polite.

I decided to act quickly.

"This is my boyfriend Malcolm," I said proudly as hell and put my arm through his.

Sean held his hand out to shake Malcolm's hand but Malcolm just looked at him. Sean put his hand back.

"It's all good bro. You won. I'm happy for y'all," he said with a condescending grin.

With a smirk, Malcolm replied, "I am not your bro and it was never a competition."

I immediately turned us to others that were waiting to speak with us. Sean walked away. We finally were able to sit and enjoy the night. After dinner and the presentations, there was a live band playing some pretty amazing music. I went to the restroom, so we could leave. As I was coming out, Sean grabbed my wrist.

"Can I talk to you real quick?"

I snatched my arm away from him.

"What's going on?" I responded.

"I just want you to know, I'm not trying to cause any problems between you and your bodyguard but I feel like you and I need closure."

I started laughing. "Closure? For what?" I asked.

"At the end of the day, Lexi you and I were friends. We were more than friends. Did you forget? If this moutherfucker didn't have money to afford your uppity ass, you would be begging me to come to tickle that sweet ass!"

"Look, you arrogant bastard, we were nothing more than friends with benefits. News flash! I now have someone else giving me those benefits real well! So the only closure I have for you is mother-fucking bye! Enjoy the rest of your night." I walked back towards my table and Malcolm wasn't there. I grabbed my wrap on the back of my chair and looked around. Malcolm was already standing by the door. I thought that was strange but I headed towards him. When I got to him, he was not looking happy. He looked like he was upset about something. "You alright baby?" I asked.

"I'm just ready to go." He responded without even looking at me.

I looked around hoping no one else heard his tone and how short he had become. We walked out of the ballroom and Tebow was waiting for us. We took the elevator down and headed towards the car pick up area. I tried to hold Malcolm's hand as we walked through the casino, and he acted like he didn't see my hand reach for him. He walked with both hands in his pockets. I used one hand to hold the bottom of my gown as I held my clutch with the other. We made it outside and Big B was standing with the back door open to the Rolls Royce Malcolm had brought to Vegas. I got in first and Malcolm followed. I wasn't in the car one second before the tears fell from my eyes. What the fuck was going on tonight?

"You care to explain to me why you had to lie to me and meet your little ex-boyfriend by the bathroom?" Malcolm asked very abruptly and out of nowhere.

You. Got. To. Be. Fucking. Kidding. Me? I thought to myself. I couldn't even talk to him because my emotions were all over the place.

"Lexi, are you going to answer me?" he asked.

I slightly turned my head and said, "I'll talk to you when we get home."

My feelings were hurt that he could treat me like this and not even ask me to explain.

~

We arrived at the house a few minutes later and I got out of the car. Malcolm went through the foyer towards the living area and I went up the stairs. I waited in the bedroom for 30 minutes thinking he would follow me upstairs, so we could talk. He never came up. "Fuck this!" I stood up, finally tired of waiting. I walked over to the closet, changed into a pair of sweatpants and a half sweatshirt. I threw my socks and tennis shoes on, grabbed my purse and headed down the stairs. Before I could get to the bottom of the stairs, Malcolm was heading up.

"Where are you going?" He asked with a slur.

His eyes looked different.

"Oh hell no!" He was drunk. "I'm going home!" I said

"Home? You're not going home! This is your home! You're going to meet that little midget ass ex boyfriend of yours. Do I look like a fool? Is this why you didn't want me to go? Why Lexi? I saw you talking to him all secretly by the restrooms. I saw you giggling and laughing with this moutherfucker. I've never felt so disrespected and embarrassed."

"You're out of your fuckin mind, X!" I blurted.

"Out of my mind?" He tripped trying to hold on to the rail at the bottom of the staircase. "I'm out of my mind for thinking I would be enough for you. I'm out of my mind for thinking you really loved me. I'm out of my mind to trust you."

I got as close as I could to Malcolm's face. I was on a stair step higher than him, so we were eye to eye. "I am going to let you live after what you just said to me because I know your lightweight ass is drunk off a few sips of alcohol. But let me tell you something, Mr. Malcolm Xavier Styles. If you don't trust me or think I don't love you, we need to end this bullshit right now."

Both of our eyes were starting to water as we looked into each other's eyes.

I explained to Malcolm that Sean approached me as I was coming out of the restroom and wanted to talk about closure. I explained to him that I told Sean to fuck off. "You actually said you don't trust me." My eyes were tearing up. "You don't get to hurt me, Malcolm. I didn't do anything to hurt you."

Malcolm tried to hold me around my waist but I didn't let him. I moved past him and went towards the door. "I'm going to my home. I need some time."

"Please don't leave me," Malcolm said. "I'm sorry, Lexi. Baby, don't leave. I'm sorry."

His eyes were glossy and he looked so sincere. My ass stayed. I didn't leave.

Chapter Twenty-Three

ALEXIS

I flew out to New York that Thursday, November 18th. Had I waited until Friday Malcolm would have been in Las Vegas. I went straight to the house and up to the bedroom. Malcolm was coming out of the shower and there I was standing in the bathroom smiling. He was happy to see me which made me even happier to be here and share the good news. Of course, we made love. This seems to be our common way of saying *hi.* Our common way of saying *I miss you.* Our common way of saying *I love you.* Our common way of just existing. And I loved every minute of it.

That night Malcolm told me how connected we both must be because he was thinking I should come to New York because he had a very important meeting on Friday and wouldn't be able to get to Vegas until late Friday or early Saturday.

We laid on the couch and watched a couple of movies and talked about Thanksgiving plans. He told me that we were invited to Drew's parent's house in New Orleans. I was excited being that I've never been to New Orleans. Malcolm told me that he had something for me and wanted to give it to me tonight. My mind went to some x-rated stuff automatically and I said "you can give it to me anytime" in a joking manner. Malcolm did a halfway smile which told me he didn't really hear my joke.

Malcolm got on one knee and pulled out a box and looked me dead in my eyes. I immediately froze. My heart was beating so hard and fast. He held my left hand. "I've had this ring for a while now. I knew the first time I met you that you would be my wife one day. I've been waiting for the perfect moment to ask you. When you showed up today, I knew it was time. You sitting here tonight in your sweats and my t-shirt, you look extremely beautiful!" He went on to say, "I love you and I believe with all my heart you love me too. I love everything that we have and I want to give you the world. I love every moment we're together and I want to have these moments for the rest of my life with you. Alexis Lynn Bell, will you marry me?"

With tears falling down my cheeks, I said, "Yes, I will marry you! Malcolm, I love you so much."

He placed the ring on my finger. I looked at it and it was the most beautiful ring I had ever seen. We kissed, and he carried me upstairs over his shoulder to the bedroom. I laughed and giggled so hard, I was so happy. This might have been the happiest moment of my life. "Thank you, God," I yelled out as he carried me upstairs.

That morning I woke up before Malcolm. I looked at my ring on my finger and decided to talk to God. I thanked God for blessing me and loving me enough to give me this much joy. He's given me the one thing I never had...my own family. I looked over at Malcolm who was sleeping so good and looking even better. I jumped on top of him and began kissing all over his face! He woke up, smiled and moved my hair out of his face! As he looked at me, I confessed. "I am so happy! You make me so happy baby! Thank you for loving me so much. I pray I make you happy!" I kissed him all over his face!

"We're just getting started, baby. My number one goal is to bring you joy every day for the rest of your life. You're mine for infinity". He then flipped me over and started kissing me and tickling me oh my god this feeling I never want it to go away. Malcolm then had to leave to go to his meeting.

~

J was so excited about tonight. I had it all planned out. I would be cooking a wonderful meal for Malcolm. I would then give him the best news ever. I had to tell him in person. I had already gift wrapped the stick and wrote a beautiful letter to let him know how I was feeling about him and our future. I had a little over 3 hours to get it all together before he returned to the house.

Moving around the kitchen was pretty easy for me. I pulled out the steaks I was cutting up the zucchini when I heard footsteps heading toward the kitchen.

"Malcolm, did you come home early?" I called out and looked towards the door.

"Hello Beautiful," He stated

I froze in my place at the same time my stomach sank to the ground. It was Scorpio standing in Malcolm's kitchen with me.

"What are you doing here?" My voice shook

"You're about to find out!" He said with that same shit face grin and headed towards me. With every step he took towards me, I took a step away from him. We were actually going around the huge counter. I was so scared. He pulled out a gun. "Stop or I'll shoot your pretty ass!" I stopped, and he came up to me and grabbed my ass and pulled me into him. I was nauseous and about to pass out when we heard shots fired in the front of the house. I screamed and was shaking uncontrollably.

The shots were coming from the front of the house. I heard at least four rounds of gunfire. Tears were running like water down my face and all I could think about was Malcolm.

Scorpio let me go as he proceeded to run towards the front of the house. I immediately ran out of the kitchen. My heart was beating so fast as I ran down the back hallway off the kitchen. I heard him looking for me. I could see the back elevator from where I was hiding and was praying it worked. I ran as fast as I could to the elevator and placed my hand on the screen. The elevator opened. At the same time, I heard and simultaneously felt three sharp burning sensations hit me in my side. The impact was so forceful that I lifted off the ground and hit the back of the elevator and my head with such force. The door had already closed.

I could hear a couple more shots fired outside the elevator. I was scared for my life. The sounds stopped and I could feel myself slowly fading out. I held my stomach and cried out because the pain was the worst I'd ever felt. I was able to crawl out of the elevator and into the camera room. I cried Malcolm's name and held my stomach as I cried for my unborn baby. I couldn't catch my breath and soon everything went out.

Chapter Twenty-Four

Malcolm

I was short of breath, as I approached the nurse's station in the ER. I couldn't hear anything or talk to anyone. I think Drew was doing the talking. I followed him as we ran through some doors to the team just as they were heading into surgery with Lexi. They didn't let me get close to her, but I was able to see her body and all the blood as they rolled her through some more doors. Through my watering eyes, I stopped a couple of doctors "That's my fiancé! Please do everything you can. Don't let her die. I'm begging you. Please!" We'll do the best we can, Son". One of them replied. They left, and I was standing there feeling helpless and alone. By now, the story was all over the news and several people from our AMS family had shown up. I remembered seeing Tebow's wife and Big B's family. I must have been a mess because Drew walked me out of the hallway and into what looked like the Chapel at the hospital.

All I kept hearing in my mind was Lexi's voice saying "I love you." I could see her perfect face and beautiful smile. She was so happy this morning. My thoughts then went to her being shot and how I was not there to protect her. What was she thinking in those moments?

Drew was right there beside me. He started praying out loud as we knelt in front of the cross in the chapel. I had never felt so defeated. After a moment of silence, I heard him tell me that Scorpio and the other two goons he had with him were dead. He told me that Tebow and Big B both had been shot and that Tebow was in surgery to remove a bullet in his leg.

After about 3 hours of me sitting in the chapel numb, the doctor came in. He sat down next to me and I looked him in his eyes. I was looking in the eyes that were identical to mine and belonged to my father. The doctor sitting here with me was my dad. I knew he was a surgeon in New York. I just never knew exactly where he worked. Dr. Malcolm Styles, MD was scripted across his white coat. An older version of me, with gray hair and glasses. I still wasn't able to formulate words. He told us that Lexi had just come out of surgery and was headed to ICU. He told me that I could see her in about 15 minutes. "*Son, the good news is that all three bullets went through her flesh and none were lodged inside of her body.*" He then said, "*there was a very small area of torn muscle that had to be stitched, and we repaired it.*" He took a deep sigh and said I'm sorry to tell you that "*Lexi lost the baby. We performed a Dilation and curettage which is a procedure to remove the tissue from the uterus. She also went into what we call a traumatic coma. She is being monitored, and we will do everything we can to help her regain consciousness.*"

I heard everything he said. She lost the baby? Lexi was pregnant? Did she know? If she knew, why didn't she tell me?

"*We have to pray, especially now. These next 24 hours are crucial.*" I saw tears sitting in his eyes. I saw Drew with his face in his hands. My dad, the surgeon, who just operated on Lexi hugged me. My entire body crumbled as I cried in his arms. "It's all my fault." I cried out. The more I cried, the tighter he hugged me. We cried in that embrace for a while. I finally got up and wiped my face with my hands. My voice was hardly recognizable, "Can I go and see her now?" I asked. "Absolutely!" He replied and then handed me a bag with Lexi's engagement ring, earrings and necklace. "I didn't want these items just lying around." He led me to her room.

∾

I entered the room alone. I walked over and saw her beautiful body looking so helpless. My insides started trembling, as I tried to control the onset of emotions I felt tugging at my heart. I hugged her and cried. I cried for Lexi and our baby. I cried seeing all the machines hooked up to her. I cried as I saw remnants of blood on her hands and face. I was overcome with emotions. I cried for Lexi. I cried for my unborn child. I cried for Tebow. I cried for Big B. I cried for my mom. I cried about seeing my dad. I cried because I felt so empty and alone. *I'm sorry baby. Please don't die. Please don't leave me.*

I was in this position for a while. A few nurses came in, and they brought in a special recliner that laid out to a twin size bed, just in case I needed it. I don't know what Dr. Styles said to the hospital staff but the preferential treatment I received was appreciated. They worked around the clock on checking her ventilator, heart monitors, and IV's. Everyone was so nice and empathetic. They brought in water and offered me food, it didn't matter to them that I declined every time. I couldn't eat or drink. Drew was allowed to come in long after visiting hours that night. When he knocked on the door and came in, he went over to Lexi's bedside and said a prayer. He then turned to me and we hugged. "I know this is rough on you and I know you're hurting. Just know that I love you man and I'm here for you. All these years you've been the strongest of the both of us and I need you to let me be the strong one now." He didn't wait on me to respond and just kept talking. He told me that I didn't have to say anything, he just needed me to listen. He told me that Tebow was doing great. His Surgery went well and he is now resting. His wife E'Marie was with him and wanted you to know that they're praying for Lexi. The doctors said he would be discharged in a day or two and back walking normally in about 4-6 weeks. Big B was released and at home. Luckily, he was wearing his bulletproof vest. He told me that he gave a statement and that they just wanted to find a motive as to why Scorpio would come on my property? The detective wanted to know about our relationship with them. They didn't need any more information because all three guys were involved in gangs and drugs. The weapons confiscated tonight were connected to 3 different homicides in New York and New Jersey. The police also had the video footage of them parking up the road and sneaking onto the property and the footage of the entire incident. He told me not to worry about anything other than Lexi. Drew took this time to tell me that he was so sorry all of this happened. I hugged him. I still couldn't really speak. He then reached in his jacket. I have these things that the detective said you might want. He handed me a gift box, a letter envelope and Lexi's cell phone. My heart was beating so fast. Drew left.

That night a nurse brought in a blanket and pillow for the recliner chair they had in the room.

I pushed the chair as close as I could to the bed. I kissed Lexi's hand and opened up my letter. My name was in cursive (I never knew how beautiful her handwriting was).

Dear Love,

If you're reading this letter, We just finished dinner, and I am sitting right across from you with the biggest smile on my face. I might even be crying from sheer joy.

Stop reading and kiss me! LOL!

You are my everything. I thank God for the love you have shown me. I will forever be grateful for our love and how God put us together. You make me so happy. Okay. Okay. 5,4,3,2,1...Malcolm, WE'RE HAVING A BABY! Yep! I'm pregnant! My Heart is about to burst because I will soon have our baby! You have given me the one thing I want more than anything...my own family! Another person on this earth with my blood and hopefully your looks. We really have a little human coming in 7 to 8 months, made from our love.

Open your gift.

P.S. This will have to hold you over until our first doctor's appointment next week on Wednesday, November 24 at 9:30 am. They said we will be able to hear the baby's heartbeat.

Congratulations, Daddy!

Love you, Lexi

I opened the gift and found the pregnancy test with a plus symbol in the little window. Tears rolled down my face as I sat there and felt pain like never before.

Chapter Twenty-Five

Malcolm

That morning, I woke up to one of the nurses checking Lexi's vitals and changing her IV bag. I asked how she was, and she just said the same. I held Lexi's hand good morning, Beautiful. I imagined her laughing and smiling at me. Seeing her lying here like this didn't seem right or real.

My dad walked in and said good morning and went straight to Lexi. He checked her vitals and wrote some things in her chart. I searched his eyes to see if I could read him. It didn't look good.

"How are you?" He asked. "I've been better", I replied. "How is she?" I asked. He said all we can do is wait at his point. "Her vitals are consistent and after what she went through her body needs time." He then put a hand on my shoulder and walked out of the room.

Within two minutes, the door opened and in walked Lexi's best friends, Evelyn and Jess. They both came in crying, introduced themselves and hugged me. They immediately went to Lexi's bedside. They were crying and asking questions. I was trying to answer as many as I could. After a while, we just all hugged and Evelyn started praying. I left them alone with her. I needed coffee. I saw my dad at the nurse's station. He came over to me and asked if

I needed something. I told him I was looking for coffee. He had me follow him. We went into his office. I could smell the coffee as soon as we walked in. He poured me a cup. I told him I like my coffee black. He just smiled. His office was huge and looked very immaculate. He had several awards, plaques on one wall. On a bookshelf, were two pictures of me. One from 9th grade and my high school graduation picture. I saw another picture of my dad, his wife and her two daughters. Last I heard both daughters had returned to New York and were living back at home.

"I miss you, Son. I think about you daily. I really wish we talked more than just on Father's Day."

"I know. I will try to do better." I got up and tried to excuse myself. "I need to go check on Lexi."

"Junior! Wait! Listen, please. I am and will always be your dad. I will always love you. When you hurt, I hurt. I read about you every chance I get, so I can know what you're up to. When I saw you and Lexi in one of those gossip columns, a few weeks ago. I was so happy for you. You looked happy, Son. You haven't really been happy since your mom passed. When I saw you last night. I damn near broke down. You are my son and no matter what, I will always be here for you and your family. Do you understand?"

"I do." I said.

"Also, Junior, I need you to start talking to Lexi. More than likely, she can hear you. Try reading to her. Maybe rub her legs and feet. We have to keep her stimulated. It is important that we get her out of that coma before it's too late. Son, if Lexi is not up soon, her chances of living will decrease."

I shook my head. "Thank you." I left with my coffee.

When I returned to the room, Jess, Evelyn, and Drew were there. They were all just sitting around. Drew had brought in coffee and breakfast sandwiches. I took a couple of bites. Everyone was engaging in small talk. They were trying to get me to go home and take a shower, rest and then come back later. I ignored them. That was never going to happen. Drew said he would be back around 4 that evening and would bring me a change of clothes and a toiletry bag. He asked if I needed anything else. I didn't. Jess and Evelyn left to check into their hotel and would be returning later as well. I asked Jess if she could call Lexi's job to let them know what was going on and her condo management to let them know and have them hold her mail. Once everyone left I called my assistant, Kim to okay whatever funds needed to be released to get my house cleaned and on the market to sell. I also had her call the hospital to let them know I was paying for all of Lexi's hospital charges. She was also bringing me my laptop and getting the bag ready for Drew to bring.

When I returned to the room. It looked like Lexi had lost some of her color. I held her hand and rubbed her hair. "*Hi, Baby. I'm here, and I am not leaving you. I really miss you and need you. I love you so much, babe.*" I bent down and kissed her cheek several times. "*Lexi, my dad told me you can hear me. Yep, I said my dad. I really struggle with what to say to him. He's the lead surgeon at this hospital. He performed the surgery on you. I don't know what to say to him.* I paused. "*You're right...I need to say thank you. Now, I just need you to come back. Please come back. I kissed her again.*"

I moved to the end of the bed and lifted the blanket. I placed my hands on her legs and then her feet and realized her feet were cold. I went out of the door and asked the nurse across from the room if she could get some socks. When I returned, I started massaging her feet. "*I love your feet.*" Looking at her feet, I remembered the first time I saw them on our first date in my hotel room. I knew then I liked her even more. She has beautiful feet and hands. In my opinion, Lexi was beautiful from head to toe, literally. The nurse came in with socks and I put them on her feet after I kissed them. I continued to rub her feet and her legs. I took my time and talked with her the entire time.

Several days now, day after day, the routine was almost the same. I would wake up and wash up. I would then wash Lexi's face and rub lotion on her face. I then grabbed a cup of coffee and just sat and waited. The nurses and doctors came in every morning to check on things and gave me any updates. The updates were always pretty much the same. We got excited one day because her eyes flickered however, she didn't come out of her coma. Another day, she moved her hands a couple of times but was still in a comatose state.

Every day, Jess, Evelyn, Drew and my dad were there at one time or another. They all formed relationships. Jess and Drew usually ran errands for food or coffee. My dad and Drew spent a lot of time talking as well. Evelyn spent a lot of time answering her phone because her husband needed her. I usually just sat and looked at Lexi. Thanksgiving came and went. My dad's wife, Dorothy cooked dinner and brought it to the hospital. We had a good day. We all sat around and ate. They shared stories and laughed a little. I found out that Lexi used to sing and was a great singer. I saw a video from two years ago where Lexi was singing at her friend's wedding. She sounded like an angel. I smiled and then my heart started hurting again. I missed her so much and couldn't explain the level that pained my heart. Each day, someone was bringing lunch or dinner to the room. I was very grateful for Jess, Evelyn and Drew. Each night I would take a shower after 9 and then rub the medication cream on Lexi's side. I always massaged her arms, legs and feet. I then held her hand until I fell asleep. Sometimes, I played music for her throughout the night.

Lexi had been in the hospital now for 10 days. Over time, Tebow and his wife came to visit. Big B, Jess and Evelyn's family from Georgia came to pray and check on her too. The crew showed up at the same time today. I noticed that Drew had started picking up Jess and Evelyn, each day. They must have arranged this earlier. Evelyn had to leave tomorrow but said she would be back as soon as she could.

That night, after dinner, my dad came in and gave us an update. He said they were hopeful when Lexi's heartbeat had increased but then it went back down. He told us that the number of days she's been in the coma was not good and that eventually, a decision would have to be made. He said that she needed our prayers more than ever right now. The girls started crying and praying instantly. I couldn't quite comprehend what he was saying and went numb again. I didn't know if I should be angry with him for coming in here with that type of negative information. I knew I would never in a million years make a decision that would take her away from me and I hope no one thought I would. Giving up on Lexi, wasn't an option for me. I would look at her in this state for the rest of my life before I did anything that would take her away from me. I didn't know if I was being unrealistic about her condition and or progress. I remember that we all prayed together and everyone left for the night. They said they would return early the next morning.

Chapter Twenty-Six

Malcolm

*A*lone with Lexi and looking at her, reality set in. The tears fell instantly. I felt helpless. I got as close as I could without actually laying my whole body on the bed. I closed my eyes and laid my forehead on her face. Through my tears and heartache, I forced my words out. "*Baby... baby, please don't leave me. I need you. You're my everything, Lexi... Can you hear me?... Baby, if you can hear me, please let me know...Lexi, you and only you make me complete. I can't even imagine you not being here with me...I finally have someone to love and I don't think I could live through another heartbreak, baby. I wish it was me that had taken the shots you took. I'm sick to my stomach every day without you. I don't want to imagine that you could leave me or this earth. Please, Lexi, come back... you told me you would never leave me.*" My sobs were uncontrollable. I held her hand and started talking to God. "*Dear God please help me. Please give Lexi the strength to come out of this coma. Please love us enough to give us life together here on earth. I need you, God. She needs you, God. Please I'm begging.*"

I felt her hand twitch. I looked up at Lexi through my tears and saw her eyes slightly open. "*Baby, can you hear me?*" She tried to squeeze my hand. I pushed the button to call the nurse. The nurse came in and had me move back. She started talking to Lexi to get her to respond. She had a little metal flashlight flickering on each of her eyes. Another nurse came in and they tried sitting her up. She kind of flopped a little then all of a sudden Lexi started having convulsions. Her eyes closed tight, and she started screaming, crying and shaking. She was crying out my name, and I was trying to get to her, but they wouldn't let me. Two male nurses had to hold me back. By now, there were at least 4 nurses and my dad working on Lexi. They gave her a shot to calm her. One of the nurses explained that Lexi had suffered a panic attack from trying to come out of her coma. They said this was normal after a traumatic event like what she had experienced. Over the next hour, they started unplugging her ventilator and her IV's. The only thing she had was an oxygen mask to even out her breathing. They told me that the heart and BP monitor had to remain at least until the morning. I was finally able to go to her. Her eyes were open but glazed over. I moved closer to her, I saw the tears running down the sides of her face. I kissed her face. I kissed her tears. I held her as tight as I could without hurting her. Through my kisses and tears, I whispered to her. "*I love you! I love you so much. Thank you for not leaving me. Thank you, God.*" Lexi was trying to talk and I removed her mask. "*Malcolm.*" She was crying. I just held her. "*I'm here baby. I will always be here. Just relax baby, you're okay.*"

"*Malcolm. My baby.*" Her tears were falling nonstop down towards her ears and on the pillow. She closed her eyes. "*It's okay, baby. It's okay. I promise.*" I whispered to her. My heart felt like it was going to explode because I loved her so much.

The nurse returned to remove her catheter. They told me that they had to get her some fluids and pain medication. Then they would keep her under observation all night. They assured me that she was only going uphill from this point on. My dad returned and I went to him with my hand out to say thank you. He just hugged me and I hugged him back.

That night Lexi slept off and on. She would rub my hand wherever she woke up. I might have gotten a total of an hour of sleep and was happy about it. My Baby was up and I knew this was just the beginning of many more blessings to come. I helped her drink the water on the tray. She was talking more. She told me she loved me. She asked me how long she had been in this place? She cried so much about losing the baby. I didn't know what to say. I just listened and comforted her the best I could.

That morning when Drew, Jess and Evelyn walked in, they were in disbelief but happy was an understatement. By afternoon, Lexi's hospital room looked like a floral shop. She was slowly returning to herself.

They were able to get her up that morning to try to walk to the bathroom. She did amazing. The hospital staff kept saying she did a 360 and was a miracle. We constantly stole looks at each other and communicated our love through our eyes. With the help of Jess and Evelyn, she was able to shower and get her hair washed and brushed. Jess had parted her hair down the middle and braided her hair in two french braids. That night she even was able to eat her soft diet meal that they brought in. Drew and Jess dropped Evelyn off at the airport that night and Jess was able to get her flight out the next morning. I was grateful for both of them and considered them family now.

After that day, Lexi had to walk as much as possible. Within 3 days, Lexi was walking at least 4 times a day up and down the hallway. I usually walked with her and held her hands each morning and right before bed. We showed our appreciation and admiration for each other through smiles, hugs, kisses, me helping her eat, get dressed, and her making sure I was as comfortable as possible. I left a couple of days for no more than a few hours each time to get things in order. I needed to stop by the office a couple of times. Meet with my Realtor at the house and sign closing paperwork. She was also scouting a penthouse in Manhattan for me. I meet with my personnel team to get everything packed, sold or donated. I even sold my cars. I had a team transport all of our clothes and belongings to Vegas. My last stop was to visit my mom.

Twenty days after the tragedy, Lexi was discharged from the hospital. She had met Dr. Styles and let's just say they were best friends at this point. He would spend at least an hour each day just sitting and talking with her when his shift ended. To be honest my heart was happy to see her and my father build this relationship. She was doing well. He said she could resume her regular activities but asked that she not lift anything over 10 lbs for 2 more weeks. They gave her permission to fly back to Las Vegas, and she already had a doctor's appointment in a few days to make sure she was still doing good.

Chapter Twenty-Seven

ALEXIS

The cold December air felt so good on my face! I hugged Dr. Styles for a long time. In his ear, I whispered, "Thank you for saving my life." He whispered back in my ear, "Thank you for coming into my life and bringing my son back to me." We embraced for a while longer and then I got in the truck. Malcolm and his dad hugged and said their good-byes. Malcolm then climbed into the truck right behind me. Drew and Big B drove us to the airport to get on our plane to Vegas. The plane was waiting and ready. It was a different plane than usual. Malcolm said he leased this plane because it had custom chaise lounges for comfort.

I'm glad he did because the flight to Vegas was the best! Malcolm and I held each other and snuggled the entire flight. We were able to lay and hold each other for hours. He had my engagement ring cleaned, and he slid it back on my finger. I loved laying on Malcolm's chest and feeling his kisses on my forehead. We both took a short nap. I missed breathing him. A few tears fell, thinking about everything that had happened.

We arrived in Vegas by 5 pm that evening. Car service took us to the condo. My condo looked like it had been vacant for a while. Everything was cleaned but it had no life. *No life.* I opened the curtains to see the night view of the city. It was bright but not as beautiful as I remembered. We went to the bedroom to shower and get ready for bed. Malcolm started the shower and helped me take off my clothes. I started crying, and he wanted to know what he could do. I told him I just needed to shower and rest. Once in the shower alone, I lost control of my emotions. My mind went back to being shot and losing my baby. I felt so alone. *My baby was gone. My biological parents gave me away. The only family I've ever had died and left me.* I closed my eyes so tight. *Why, God?* The pain I was feeling, jolted my insides. With my hands covering my mouth as I shook and curled up in the corner of the shower, I silently cried until my chest hurt. I couldn't control my crying any longer. Something from deep down in my soul was fighting to escape. Through my tears, I let out the most horrifying cry. I don't think I've ever cried like this in my life. Malcolm was in the shower with his clothes on holding me. I apologized to Malcolm for losing our baby. I cried and told him how sorry I was for everything. He picked me up and carried me to the bed. We wrapped up in the blankets. I held on to him as he comforted me and let me cry. I cried myself to sleep.

The next morning, I woke up alone in the bed. Malcolm was up and in the kitchen. He had ordered breakfast and was working on his laptop. As soon as he heard me place my glass of water down on the nightstand, he came back into the room. The good morning kiss he gave me made my whole body come alive.

"Mmmmhm, Good morning." I said

"Good morning, Beautiful." He said

"Come eat. I made you some hot tea." I got up, put my robe on and went to wash up and brush my teeth. I noticed that the sun was shining so bright and beautiful. As we ate our veggie omelet and fresh fruit, we made small talk about Christmas being only two weeks away. We talked about my job and my decision to take a leave of absence. We both agreed that was the best decision right now.

Malcolm turned towards me while still sitting on his barstool, "Lexi, I would like to talk to you about our wedding."

I took a sip of my tea and asked, "What about our wedding?" I kept a brave face but I felt like I was going to faint. Had he changed his mind?

"Honey, what kind of wedding do you want? He asked. I thought about it and without looking up, I replied, "The only wedding I want is the one where I say I do to you for the rest of my life."

Malcolm stopped eating and put his fork down. He stood up and turned the barstool I was sitting on around to face him. Standing between my thighs, he placed a hand on the side of my face and asked "How much time do you need to plan a wedding where you say I do to me for the rest of your life?"

I got as close as I could to his mouth. "All I want is to become your wife and nothing more."

I didn't think we could get any closer, but he did. Our lips were as close as they could get to each other, without touching. "Are you saying you would marry me right now and bypass walking down the aisle, white dress, family and friends?"

"I'm saying I want to be your wife now more than anything. I don't have a father to walk me down the aisle and you're my family. Marrying you right now is what I want more than anything in this world."

We finally let our lips touch. His mouth felt so strong as he kissed me passionately. There was so much love and emotion between us. I wanted him so bad that I was close to tears. "The world is yours, baby!" He whispered. He then said, "get yourself beautiful because we're getting married today!" We both smiled and hugged. Malcolm picked me up as we continued to hug. He gave me a quick kiss on the cheek and said let's go!

I went to the spa to get my hair, nails, toes, eyebrows, eyelashes, and wax done. He went to run errands. I went to my closet and picked out a beautiful off-white St. John knit dress with a thin satin tie around the waist. The dress came with a sweater coat. I paired it with a pair of 4 inch jimmy choo shimmer gold pumps. My hair was in loose curls with a side part. I was pleasantly surprised how my hair came out being that I had it done at the spa, and they knew nothing about straightening black hair. Malcolm chose a pair of black tailored slacks, black dress shirt and black Louboutins. He went to the barber. His hair and beard were trimmed, and he looked even more handsome. Before we left, a jeweler and a notary came to the condo. One had paperwork and the other had several cases of wedding sets. Both of us signed the paperwork then We picked out a beautiful platinum set. Malcolm's ring was solid platinum with a titanium inset. My band was full of diamonds to match the 10-carat engagement ring I was already wearing. The driver picked us up from the condo at about 6:45 pm. We drove up Las Vegas Boulevard and decided we would just pick a random chapel that we both agreed on.

Chapter Twenty-Eight

ALEXIS

The Wedding Bell Chapel was perfect! As soon as we walked in, I noticed a few beautiful flower crowns. Malcolm bought one for me and placed it on my head with a kiss to the forehead. He paid whatever fees we owed, and we were led into a small beautiful room filled with white roses surrounding us. The room was breathtaking. We both expressed an indescribable feeling. The minister prayed with us, and then we shared our vows as we held hands. I was already crying as I looked at him and said what was on my heart.

"My Dearest Malcolm, this is the happiest day of my life. When I look at you and especially right now, I see love like I've never known. You make every day feel like a dream to me. Your love for me is the reason I'm alive today." Never letting go of my hand, Malcolm used his thumb to wipe away my tears. I continued. "Today I'm giving you my whole heart because I trust you and only you with it. I promise to love you until the end of time. There is no me without you and I will never leave you. God will always be our guide and you will always be my King. I love you forever, Malcolm Xavier Styles."

Malcolm kissed my hand. His beautiful eyes were holding a tear in each as he took a deep breath. "Alexis, today I'm marrying the love I've been missing all my life. You've come into my life and given me exactly what I need. In this world, what matters to me the most is you and always will be. I feel like I'm in a dream as well, Babe. I promise you loyalty and love all my days. With that loyalty and love, I could never hurt you. I promise to give you every part of me and trust you with my heart. Wherever you are is where I want to be. I never want to be apart from you, Lexi. Thank you for being my heaven on earth. I promise to always take care of you and keep you safe. Other than God, as your husband, I hope to supply all your wants and needs. I promise to give you the world that you deserve. I love you, Alexis Lynn."

The minister said more things and something about the state of Nevada, etc before he announced that we were husband and wife. We kissed for the first time as man and wife. They took pictures, we received a video and a chapel certificate of marriage. The certificate said on top, "What God has joined together as one, let no one or nothing pull it apart."

That night we stopped by a private tattoo artist. I had *MALCOLM* tatted going down my side opposite of the side I was shot. Before the M and after the M in his name was a black heart. Infinity symbols connected the letters. He tatted *ALEXIS* on his chest and over his heart and finished his second sleeve on his right arm with my name outlined on an infinity symbol. We got bandaged up really good and left. While driving down the Las Vegas strip, we called all our friends and family to share our news. We took pictures and kissed as much as we could. We went to a club inside the Bellagio Hotel Casino. We were seated in a VIP section where we took a sip of champagne, kissed, danced and enjoyed ourselves. I felt like I was dreaming. I asked Malcolm to pinch me. Was I alive and was this real. He said "hell yeah you're alive and I'm going to make sure you always feel like you're dreaming. Welcome to your new reality, Mrs. Styles." We kissed and gently swayed back and forth. We made a toast that night. *to us*. The club announced Mr. and Mrs. Styles just got married. Everyone cheered, and we drank a few more sips of champagne. The alcohol helped me endure the pain I was experiencing from my new tattoo. Malcolm told me that night in the club that we had a suite there tonight, and he had everything we needed in the suite. Before we left the club, the news was all over the internet and social media. That night I made love to my husband for the first time. Malcolm and I made the most beautiful love we've ever made. We couldn't get buck wild because I felt like I was cut in half from my tattoo. Malcolm didn't even feel his tattoo. Both of us took a sleeping pill and fell asleep holding each other. The next day we ordered room service a few times and stayed in bed. We laughed and reminisced about our very first date in this same suite. Malcolm asked me to sing for him. He shared with me that he heard me sing on a video. He told me he thought my voice was beautiful. At first, I said, no then I said, "I will sing some lyrics and you name the artist, okay?" he agreed and I started. I decided to sing a little Jill Scott for him. With my eyes closed, I sat up and sang Acapella as he sat up and watched.

Your hands on my hips pull me right back to you... I catch that thrust, give it right back to you... You're in so deep, I'm breathing for you... You grab my braids, arch my back high for you...You're diesel engine, I'm squirting mad oil..Down on the floor 'til my speaker starts to boil...I flip shit, quick slip, hip dip and I'm twisted... In your hands and your lips and your tongue tricks...And you're so thick and you're so thick and you're so..Crown Royal on ice, crown royal on ice...Crown Royal on ice, crown royal on ice...

As soon as I finished, Malcolm jumped up "Woooah! First of all, you singing a Jill Scott song got me on a hundred! Lexi, you've been holding out on me this whole time!" He pulled the belt loose on my robe and gently pulled me to him. "What made you sing that song?" He asked. I smiled, "you." I replied. Malcolm used the back of his four fingers and rubbed the down one side of my cheek. "I hope you know that I love you more than anything in this world." I stole a quick kiss as he asked me if I could sing to him some more. *Am I Dreaming* by Atlantic Starr was the song I chose to sing.

Things are kind of hazy... And my head's all cloudy inside... Now I've heard talk of angels... I never thought I'd have one to call mine... See you are just too good to be true...And I..hope...this is not some kind of mirage with youuu... Am I dreaming...Am I just imagining you're here in my life... Am I dreaming.. Pinch me to see if it's real cause my mind can't decide...Will this last for one night... Or do I have you for a lifetime... Please say that it's forever...And that it's not an illusion to my eyes...And I..hope... that you don't run out and disappear... My love... I pray... that it's not a hoax and it's for real...

When I opened my eyes on the last note, a tear fell and my body was somewhat trembling. I saw Malcolm was holding tears in his eyes. We embraced and I said, "I love you more than anything in this world too." We loved each other and laid around the rest of the day. Malcolm and I talked about our future. He asked me if I want to live in our big house or our condo? I laughed because I loved that he said, *Ours*. And of course, I'm going to choose *Our* big house. We stayed another night at the hotel. *It was just us.* I felt so complete and loved.

~

The next day we went to my doctor's appointment first. The doctor was very thorough and gave me a good follow-up report. She even gave me topical pain cream for my tattoo. We then went straight to *our* big house. Ms. Rita and Mr. Gene were so happy to see me and the feeling was mutual. I helped Malcolm hire them over two months ago to live and work at the house. They had a whole casita attached to the west side of the property. They were the nicest people. Ms. Rita helped me use my Spanish and I helped her with her English. They had lunch prepared for us. They even had a wedding gift for us. It was a beautiful wedding photo album. I found out Malcolm had stopped by here since our return to Vegas.

Being in the house was surreal. This home was so beautiful and felt so safe. I thoroughly enjoyed decorating it and was going to enjoy making it my home even more. Malcolm came up behind me while I was walking around. "Welcome home, Mrs. Styles."

"Yes, I love the sound of that."

"What kind of Christmas tree do you want?" He asked.

"I can't even imagine what kind of tree for this house," I said. "Do you think you'll like a white tree with silver ornaments?" I asked.

"Yes. That sounds good to me." We had dinner, took a bath together, and went to bed early that night.

That next morning, I woke up to a lot of noise inside and outside the house. After washing up and putting on my robe, we went downstairs and a 20-foot white Christmas tree was being put up in the great room. Malcolm asked me to open the front door. I opened the front door to get a glimpse of the trucks and men outside putting lights on all the palm trees around the property. I was so excited about all the work going on at the house today. My eyes went straight to the half circle parking area/driveway to the left of the front door. *What the fuck?* I whispered to myself as I exited the front door and walked toward the parking area and six car garage. There was a new Lamborghini, Escalade, Rolls Royce, Mercedes G Wagon and a Porsche Panamera. The Mercedes and the Porsche had huge red bows on them. I turned around and Malcolm was standing there smiling. "I couldn't decide on which to get you, so I got both of them for you. I hope you like them." I ran and jumped on him and said thank you! "Why?" I asked. "A wedding gift for my wife." He said as he kissed me. He put me down "I love them and I love you. This shit is insane!" I said. We kissed again and then headed over to check out each vehicle. I was giddy as hell. I had never been in cars like these. After getting in each one, we finally went inside the house to get dressed for the day. I was excited about driving one of the cars to the store to purchase holiday decorations for the house. I picked out a suede black shirt dress to wear. I completed the dress with my Prada riding boots and Prada hat. I had already decided to drive the Mercedes G Wagon.

I checked my account before I left and saw over five million dollars in my account. I screamed "Malcolm!" He came running out the closet with no shirt on and his towel around his waist from the shower. "What's wrong?"

"Malcolm, Why do I have five million dollars in my account?" My eyes were widened and staring intently at him. I'm sure I looked nervous because my insides felt nervous. "Shit!" I added.

Malcolm spoke softly. "You're my wife. I transferred it 2 days ago, right before our wedding. Are you really upset?"

I didn't want to seem ungrateful and Malcolm had a look where his eyebrows were scrunched up in confusion. "I'm not upset, but that's a lot of money for one person...Right?" I paused and waited for him to say something. His eyebrows were still scrunched up as well as he started rubbing his head. I went towards him, to get closer. "What do you want me to buy with all that money, baby?"

"I want you to buy whatever you want." He looked me directly in my eyes. In a loving tone, he continued. "I don't ever want you to want for anything. I want you to get whatever your heart desires. Lexi, that's *your* money in *your* account. Please don't be upset about it." He started moving towards me. "I have a lot of money and now I have a wife who has a lot of money." As he stood close to me, he removed his towel. I looked down and instantly got heated. I said stop but damn I didn't mean it. He started kissing me until my back was against the wall leading to the bathroom. "You happy?" he asked as he kissed on my neck. "Ummhmmm," I moaned as I enjoyed his kisses. "Please don't question me about money again unless you need some, deal?" He had his hand under my dress and made his way between my legs. I couldn't move nor did I want to. My underwear came off, then my dress was pulled up. In one motion I was calling out his name as I wrapped my legs around him. The entire time we fucked up against the wall, I said *yes* to all types of shit spoken by him. Malcolm made it clear that *I was Mrs. Styles and I had to accept, embrace and enjoy my new lifestyle. Period.*

That evening as I came up the hill and through our property gates. I took in the most magical entrance I had ever seen. My heart was so full and ready for the holiday with Malcolm. The lights were all white and were lined perfectly on all the palm trees leading up to the house. Once I parked, Malcolm was outside to help me with all the stuff I bought. Mr. Gene was helping as well. I walked into the house and was mesmerized by the larger than normal white Christmas tree. It was as tall as the second floor with the prettiest assortment of silver ornaments on it.

That night we decorated the inside of the house, laughed and danced around. The best thing about us at home together was how we enjoyed playing music several hours a day. Each room had the system intercom, so we were able to turn the music up or down depending on our mood. We sang slow songs and rap songs to each other. We slow danced and dirty danced with each other. We cooked to music, made love to music and sometimes sparked conversations from lyrics. That night we ate ice cream on the sofa, sat and stared at the tree for hours. We both shared how Christmas was our favorite holiday. "Outside of Christmas my second favorite holiday is Thanksgiving." I shared. "My second favorite is the Fourth of July." He added. Malcolm talked about Christmas when he was younger and how his mom always made the holiday special for him and his dad. He told me that tonight watching me turn our home into Christmas reminded him of his mom. He shared so many things about her. He said his dad was always laughing with his mom and cooked a huge crab boil every Christmas Eve. Since my discharge from the hospital, Malcolm and his dad had talked at least two times. My heart was so happy for them and their renewed relationship.

A couple of days later, Malcolm told me that he had to go to New York for his company holiday party and a few other things. He was hesitant about asking me if I was comfortable going back to New York with him, but didn't want me to do something I wasn't ready for. I told Malcolm, "As long as you're with me, I feel safe." I was actually excited about going to New York with my husband during the holiday. Malcolm was happy too. He extended his 2 day solo trip to a 6-day mini staycation with his wife. We would return on Christmas Eve. This was a perfect trip, already!

Chapter Twenty-Nine

ALEXIS

*W*e checked into our suite at the Langham Hotel in Manhattan early that morning. With the full agenda we had planned this week starting tonight for Drew's all-white holiday party, we were excited to be here. Tomorrow night was the AMS East Annual Holiday Formal. Malcolm had work to do at the office and I had gifts and shopping to get done. We also had to make sure we had dinner with Dr. Styles, visit the gravesite and look at some penthouse properties with the Realtor. This was sure to be an unforgettable trip.

We put our bags in the suite and as much as we wanted to relax, we immediately went back out the door. It was beyond colder than I had expected and made sure to purchase a hat, gloves and scarf set at one of the little shops in the lobby. We had lunch at an Italian restaurant right next to the hotel, where we enjoyed pizza and salad. We then went by the gravesite and took flowers. That evening Dr. Styles and Dorthy, his wife, met us at a steakhouse in Manhattan for dinner. Malcolm had reached out to his dad and planned the dinner. Having dinner with them tonight turned out to be the best! The guys talked about their similarities, sports and politics. Listening to them made my heart full. I learned a lot about baby Malcolm and teenage Malcolm. Malcolm smiled several times throughout dinner. On our way back to the hotel, Malcolm admitted that he was happy seeing his dad and Dorothy as happy as they were. He also admitted that he really missed having his dad in his life.

We made it back to the hotel. Malcolm turned the fireplace on in our suite as soon as we returned because the temperature outside was steadily decreasing. He then turned on some jazz music followed by some old school music. We started our two-stepping then slow dancing. We made love and then took a bath together in the large whirlpool.

We took turns bathing one another and enjoying the time we still had. He sat quietly while I lathered his body up, I enjoyed catering to him, it felt natural.

He grabbed my hand and turned to look at me, "Thank you for choosing me. I love you, girl."

"Thank you, Husband." Nothing could ruin this.

We were out of the bath and unpacking when the doorbell to our suite rang. I suspiciously looked at Malcolm not knowing who that could be. He just shrugged his shoulders, which confirmed he was up to something. I went to the door and to my surprise, it was the design team from Saks 5th Avenue with two racks of clothes and cases of accessories. Malcolm had arranged for them to come, so I could pick out some real coats and thicker boots. There were several outfits as well. He didn't feel like I was prepared for the east coast weather. I knew nothing about New York winter. I picked out a black fur. I also picked out a Gucci navy and red cashmere coat with the matching knee-high heel boots and a cream cashmere and fur coat. They paired every coat with an outfit. Malcolm had a couple of items on the rack as well. I just looked at him and shook my head. I'm the luckiest wife in the world!

During our first shopping trip in New York, Malcolm had picked out an off-white long sleeve jumpsuit. The one piece had a stretch lace top and sleeves. The material in the lace was designed to cover my nipples as well as other areas on my stomach and back. Side boob and Malcolm's name was visible for all to see. The bottom half of the one piece was wide legged and satin material. It fit to perfection. This jumpsuit complimented my curves. I loved it! I wore open toe gold Louboutin heels. I wore my hair straight with a part down the middle with several gold design pins on one side. Malcolm wore his classic black slacks and black dress shirt with no tie. He finished it off with an off-white Gucci sports coat. Complete with his black Gucci dress boots.

"You look good, baby," I said. "Oh yeah, how good?" He replied. He had this extra fine ass smile on his face. So me feeling myself, decided to fuck with him. I looked him straight in his eyes, licked my lips and said, "You look good enough for me to say fuck this party and sit on your face for the rest of the night." Malcolm got so serious and matched my bullshit. He didn't even hesitate and started taking off his jacket. "You ain't said shit, Mrs. Styles!" He was trying to back me up towards the bed.

I had to stop and tell him I was just playing."Malcolm! What the hell. I was just fucking with you. Why are you so nasty?" He was trying not to laugh and just smiled.

"You remember that! You'll see how nasty I am tonight when you're sitting on my face screaming my name." I was already antici- pating returning to our suite tonight!

⁓

We walked in Drew's mansion and everyone yelled "Surprise!" unbeknownst to us, it was a wedding party for us. I was in shock, surprised and happy. All the guests at the party had on black and the house was adorned with wedding and Christmas decor. As we walked in Drew announced "Introducing Mr.and the one, the only Mrs. X Styles!" Everyone laughed and clapped, I hugged everyone and almost started crying when I saw Tebow and Big B. We hugged each other and I kissed them both and whispered, "thank you."

I was introduced to people I hadn't met before. Everyone was so kind to me. There were so many people here! Drew was loud and already drunk. We hadn't been in the house for 30 minutes, and I heard him on the mic, on the stairs and across the room telling everyone, "My boy X fell in love and married Lexi with her pretty self!" I had heard that exact statement at least 8 times all around the party. He made me laugh just by the way he talked. I heard his Louisiana accent for the first time. Malcolm and I circulated the house and said "thank you" as everyone congratulated us. "Congratulations, you two are so beautiful together, so happy for you two, oh my, you're gorgeous!" I was introduced to so many people, I knew I wouldn't remember names. You could tell Malcolm was loved and respected by his friends at the label and all the people here tonight. I saw Carla, and we hugged and gave compliments, the conversation was a little more forced than I would've imagined. I was quickly pulled in another direction by Malcolm. We left her standing by herself. Malcolm led me back to the front of the house. I was wrapped in Malcolm's arms as we leaned against the main staircase showing PDA and moving to the music. The music stopped all of a sudden. We then heard Drew's voice on the microphone. "Can I get everyone's attention? How is everyone doing tonight? Merry Muthafuckin Christmas everybody! Everyone was laughing. Drew was holding up a glass. "We're all here tonight to celebrate my boy X... Malcolm X Styles and his pretty, beautiful, classy...did I say fine wife Lexi. Hi Lexi! He lifted his glasses to us. My brother fell in love." He put his drink down and pinched the corners of his tear ducts to keep from crying. "My boy fell in love and married Lexi. Ain't she pretty y'all?" Malcolm and I were laughing. We both grabbed a glass of champagne off the tray as the server passed by us. Drew was still talking on the mic and I knew then my boy was in love." Big B went to get Drew and Tebow got on the mic. Big B helped Drew off the stage as he stated "I'm just so happy." Tebow took over. "Hello everyone! Like Big Boss Drew said we're here tonight to celebrate X and Lexi. We all know X, and we all know him as a no nonsense dude. I've been his boy since we were 18 at NYU. He put the "s" in serious. Let me tell y'all when this brother is happy he's not smiling. When he's really happy, you might get the corner of his mouth in what looks like a smile." Everyone was agreeing and chuckling. "He doesn't drink. He doesn't smoke. He doesn't dance. He doesn't date. No disrespect to his queen, Lexi, but we all know X had all the females trying to get at him. He never claimed anybody. Then one day, We were out in Vegas and I picked him up at the airport and met Lexi. This dude was smiling. Y'all hear me? Smiling. Ear to ear! I don't know about no one else but I love seeing this side of him. We love you, Boss and Lexi, we all love you too! You have made my brother the happiest any of us have ever seen. Cheers to you both for many years of happiness." Everyone was cheering and clapping. I kissed Malcolm and he kissed me back.

The DJ played a slow song, and we danced in the middle of the floor. I felt like we were the only two people in the room. I wrapped my arms around his neck as he held me around my waist and held me close. "I love you." He said in my ear. " I love you more." I said as I kissed his neck. After our slow dance, everyone clapped, and we thanked them. Well, I did. Malcolm was inhaling the side of my face and ear. I giggled because I remembered he had a glass or two of champagne. The DJ put on a classic old school jam and almost the entire house was dancing, Us included. This night was perfect! Drew and Malcolm started dancing with all their boys in the middle of the floor. I went over to the side banister again. Carla came over to me. "I just wanted to tell you that you two look gorgeous togeth-er," she said. "Thank you," I replied. "How have you been?" I asked. "I've been good. Just enjoying the fruits of my labor and waiting on Drew to grow up!"

"Oh..." I replied as I turned my head and took a sip of my drink.

She giggled. "I'm sorry. He just frustrates me sometimes." We talked a little more before Malcolm came back and put his arms around my waist. He started nibbling on my ear. I just closed my eyes and enjoyed the affection. I soon remembered Carla was standing there but when I opened my eyes she was gone.

We stayed about an hour more before we left. I was starting to feel tired and Malcolm had 4 to 5 sips more of champagne. I said goodbye to everyone as he hugged everyone on the way out the door. Big B drove us back to the hotel. That morning we slept in. Malcolm went into the office while I relaxed and talked on the phone with Jess and Evelyn. I gave them the rundown on what happened the night before. They had read and shared pictures of me on social media. My outfit was a hot topic. We laughed and caught up.

That night, The AMS party was nothing short of spectacular. Not only was I on the arm of my husband. I was on the arm of the CEO of the label. At our table were Drew and Carla, Dr. Styles and Dorthy, and Kim and her date.

The ballroom was decorated with Christmas lights, ice sculptures and human size ornaments all around the room. Malcolm and I wore all black. He wore a tuxedo and I wore a sequined form fitted gown. I pulled my hair up into a fancy ponytail.

After dinner, Malcolm was up most of the night. He acknowledged several employees and talked about AMS West. Everyone seemed excited. His staff congratulated him on his marriage and had me stand. Everyone clapped and whistled. Malcolm was all over the place that night. I talked with Dr. Styles most of the night. Carla was just sitting there scrolling through her phone. Several people from the party last night came to the table to say hello. It was good seeing them and saying thank you. Malcolm came to the table every chance he got. The only problem was that when he came so did groups of people and everyone wanted pictures. I decided to go over and look at the pictures on the wall. They made a year in review of the label. I recognized people from last night. I recognized Drew and Malcolm. They weren't lying, Malcolm didn't have one smile in any of the pictures. *That's my husband*! I had to laugh.

"I just want to say congratulations on your marriage to Malcolm." I turned and saw a female smiling at me. She was pretty. She was mixed Asian and black. Her hair was jet black and straight back but with a high Mohawk bun. "Thank you!" I said. "Hi, I'm Channel." She introduced herself.

"Hi, Channel. I'm Lexi" We shook hands. I noticed she was pregnant. "Oh wow... When are you due?" I asked. "I'm actually due any day now"

"Really? Your stomach is perfect. You look amazing to be getting ready to deliver. Good luck to you and the birth of your baby." I said as I smiled at her. My heart felt heavy for some reason. I think I thought for a brief moment about the baby I lost.

"Are you okay?" Channel asked.

"I'm fine," I replied. "Nice meeting you. Enjoy the rest of your night." I added as I walked away.

I headed back to my table but was cut off by Malcolm. "Where have you been baby?" He held me close.

"I was checking out pictures." We stole a quick kiss, and he pulled me on the dance floor. He held me close and I just placed my face close to his neck and inhaled his scent. We rocked back and forth of a song that was so seductive and beautiful.

"I love you so much," he whispered in my ear.

"I love you the most," I whispered back. We shared a kiss. I saw the flashing of pictures being taken.

Dr. Styles and his wife left a little before midnight. We would be seeing them for dinner in a couple of days. Carla moved closer to me and we caught up. Whew she could talk! I found out that she wanted Drew to commit to her, but he hadn't yet. She told me how he always bought her jewelry and expensive gifts. She shared that he would go days without talking to her then call and be attached for a day or two, then he would disappear again. She did say she was going home with him for Christmas. Apparently, she was close to his parents. She then asked me if I had ever seen Drew with another female. I acted like I didn't hear her. She asked me again.

I turned toward her and spoke, "Look, Carla, I just met you and I think you're very nice but I don't get involved in other people's affairs. I would never ask you to get involved in mine. Please respect my position in your life, respect my position in Drew's life and especially, my position and love with Malcolm." A tear fell down her cheek and she wiped it.

"You're right. I'm sorry." She went back to her phone. I felt sad for her.

"I really hope you understand, Carla," I said.

Malcolm had come over to the table and asked if I was ready? I said bye to Carla and wished her a great holiday. We hugged and Malcolm and I left a little after 1 am. It was starting to snow, and I was beyond exhausted. The suite was extremely warm when we walked in, and we stripped out of our clothes and climbed into the huge bed. We slept and cuddled all night. That morning, Malcolm kissed my cheek, told me he'd be right back before I could even wake up. I had planned on shopping a little today but the snow and cold weather made me want to stay in the bed.

Chapter Thirty

Malcolm

I got in the truck and Drew pulled off. It was a little after 9:30 am. That morning Drew texted me 911 around 8 am. I got up and went into the living area of the suite. Lexi was sound asleep. Drew told me that Channel had her baby last night and it's all over the media that I was the father of her baby. My heart stopped. We had already placed a couple of calls to one of our attorneys, and we were meeting him at a lab to get a paternity sample taken. Our attorney needed it done ASAP. He was then going to head over to the hospital with legal paperwork. I could hardly breathe thinking about Lexi and how she was going to handle this. At the lab, they took blood and DNA swabs. We left and stopped to get coffee. The snow was really coming down. Drew and I talked about how I would handle this especially with Lexi. We both agreed that I had to tell her and I had to tell her quickly.

"This is going to break her heart," Drew said.

"I know," I replied.

"Her best friend Jess texted me about 30 minutes ago asking me to call her. I know it's about what's all over social media." Drew stated. "I'll wait to return her call until later."

"I hope I'm not too late" Malcolm barely spoke." I know the

results are going to come back negative. I just need Lexi to believe me."

"I think she will. You guys really love each other and real love always prevails." Drew said.

Pulling up to the hotel, I thanked Drew and told him I'd hit him up later that day. He said he was heading home to sleep off his hangover.

~

*W*alking into the hotel, my heart was pounding. I had to tell the love of my life about this. She has been through enough bullshit behind me already. I pray she understands and forgives me. Lexi is tough, she will probably take it better than I expect.

I returned to the suite and Lexi was up and sitting on the couch with a blanket over her while watching the television. She smiled as soon as I walked in. I handed her the Latte I picked for her and kissed her lips.

"You're the best, babe!" She flashed those eyes and smiled at me. *I was about to lose my shit thinking about what was about to come.* My heart was beating so fast that my chest hurt. I placed my right hand over my heart. "What's wrong baby? Come sit." She wanted me to get comfortable and join her under the throw. I remained standing. "Lexi, I have to tell you something important." She was taking sips of her drink and stopped. She immediately went into panic mode. She stood up. "What's wrong, Malcolm? What is it?" She had no idea and her eyes were already gathering water in them. "Listen, baby, please. I love you and I need you to know it's not true." She started rocking and trying to control her breathing. "Baby tell me!" She pleaded. I looked her dead in her eyes. "Lexi a woman is claiming that I am the father of her newborn baby." The tears were falling from Lexi's face, and she was just standing there. I felt like shit. "Baby look at this," as I handed her my phone, so she could see the headlines and articles. I attempted to wipe her tears and hug her. Lexi put her hand up to stop me from touching her. "Who is she to you?" She didn't even blink. I've never seen Lexi this upset. "Her name is Channel," I answered. Feeling low and sad.

"That's not what I asked you! Who the fuck is she to you?" Lexi was shouting.

"She ain't shit to me! I hardly know her." I answered, now feeling guilty about something that was nothing.

Lexi zoomed in on a picture while reading the articles on my phone.

She looked up at me with tears coming down her face. "Was she at the AMS party last night?" Lexi asked. I shook my head, "yes." I whispered. "This bitch approached me and had a discussion with me at the party last night! I complimented her and wished her well on her baby! I must have looked like a fucking idiot! Lexi was shouting and crying at the same time. "I'm in love with a womanizing gigolo and sharing laughs with his side bitch" She started pacing and crying. I watched as Lexi started almost hyperventilating again.

"Lexi stop" I approached her. "Listen to me, it's not my baby."

She stopped and asked, Did you fuck her, Malcolm?"

"Yes...but baby I really don't think it's my baby" "I went this morning to meet with my attorney. We drew up some paperwork and I took a paternity test. I will know within 24-48 hours."

Lexi went into our room and sat on the bed. She was hugging herself, rocking and sobbing. I spent the next 30 minutes trying to talk with her or get her to talk with me. She just ignored me. I felt like shit. I sat in the chair in the room. I kept looking at her and wondered what she was thinking. Lexi came and stood over me. "Tell me every fucking detail about you and this bitch."

I looked at her and prayed to God that I didn't leave out anything because the look in my baby's eyes was one that I had never seen. I asked if I could hold her hand, and she said "no" as she moved back, so I couldn't touch her.

"The woman is an Instagram model and goes by the name ChannelDinero. She sent me one or two dm's way before I met you"

"Direct messages about what?" Lexi asked.

My head was spinning. I refuse to lie to Lexi, and she was all in my face. *Fuck.* "How she hated she missed running into me at a couple of club appearances. I entertained her and said maybe next time. We finally met face to face in February at one of my label parties at my house. She...I let her...well give me..."

"Give you what, Malcolm? You let her give you head?"

"Yeah"

"Then what?"

"She left."

"Then what?"

"I saw her again on my birthday at a party."

"Your birthday is in March Malcolm and it's December! That's for 9 months! Fuck you, Malcolm!" Lexi started crying again and asked through her sobs, "what happened on your birthday?"

"When she asked the question, she could barely get the word birthday out because she was crying. "Lexi, I went to the bathroom with her, and she did what she did the last time. I then used a condom and turned her around. I didn't come inside of her nor the condom. She finished me off orally. Lexi, there is no way her baby is mine."

We stared at each other for a while and Lexi grabbed her cell-phone and went into the second bedroom. She closed the door.

Chapter Thirty-One

ALEXIS

I looked at my phone and had 4 missed calls from Jess and 2 from Evelyn. I called Jess back. As soon as she answered, I couldn't contain myself. Through my sobbing "Jess! I'm so hurt!"

"Sis, I already know. I was trying to call you. Where is Malcolm? Please don't cry." I couldn't answer for about 3 minutes. I just cried and cried. "He's here. I read what everyone was saying about him and her. I saw the pictures of us. I feel like a fool." I feel like my beautiful love and marriage is a fuckin lie."

"You're no fool! You're in love with your husband." "Remember, all this happened before you even met him." "Malcolm would never hurt you." Do you know what you are going to do, Lexi? Do you need me to come to you?"

Malcolm says it's not his baby but I really want to talk to her." I said. Within a minute, Jess found out where she was and texted me the name and address of the hospital. I looked at the text and knew what I had to do.

"I love you, Jess. Thank you! Please pray for us. I'll call you later." I ended the call.

I came out of the room to Malcolm sitting on the floor by the door of the room I was just in. Without acknowledging him, I walked past him and into the other room. I was dressed within 15 minutes. I threw on a pair of jeans and a navy turtleneck. I had the navy and red Gucci boots and coat to match. My hair was up in a ponytail with a part down the middle. I grabbed my purse.

"Lexi, where are you going?" I heard as I was leaving out the door. "I'll be back." I paused as I saw his eyes. "I promise." I left. I threw on my oversized sunglasses. There was no sun shining outside or in my world right now. The tears rolled down as I approached the Uber. We were there within 25 minutes.

"Hello, Channel." I removed my glasses. She was sitting on the bed and the baby was next to her in her hospital bassinet. She was scrolling on her cellphone. The room was adorned with several pink balloons and flowers. Without looking back up, she said "Just so you know, I'm not accepting anything less than 1 million in my account by tonight and $10,000-$20,000 a month for child support."

"What are you talking about?" I squinted my eyes and asked.

"Look you know and I know, you don't want the embarrassment of your perfect marriage tainted by a baby. I will gladly sign an NDA with my million and monthly payments. I can raise my baby by myself." The baby started crying and Channel picked her up. She held her and I could clearly see her beautiful face.

"Channel, I'm not really sure why I came here but now that I'm here, let me let you in on a few things." I crossed my arms across my chest and my jaw was tight! "For starters, Malcolm nor I would never pay a bitch hush money to keep a child of his a secret. A secret that you have already told the world. Secondly, if this is my husband's baby we're going to do what we need to do as parents. Lastly, if this is not my husband's child, I'm fucking you up on sight the next time I see you. I put my sunglasses back on. "Congratulations and Good luck!" I left her room and headed out of the hospital. I heard the cameras. The Uber was still waiting for me. I was out sooner than I anticipated.

When I opened the suite door, Malcolm was sitting on the couch where I was earlier, and he looked miserable. Without looking at him, "Any news on the results?" I asked quietly. "Not yet." He said. I removed my coat and went over to the bar and poured me a shot of tequila.

Malcolm came over, placed his hands on my waist and turned me around to face him. "Lexi, I'm sorry." He whispered. His eyes were so fucking beautiful and sincere.

"Sorry about what, Malcolm?" I asked. I needed to hear.

"I'm sorry, I hurt you. I'm sorry you're having to live through my past actions."

I took my shot of tequila. I turned to face Malcolm. "I love you." Tears fell down my face. Malcolm grabbed me and hugged me so tight. I hugged him back. It took me a minute to catch my breath from crying.

"You're my everything, Lexi and I need you more than ever now. Please forgive me for being the way I was before you came in my life." Malcolm just let me cry as he held me. "I know you went to the hospital. I just hope you didn't believe anything she said. I need you to believe me and not leave me."

I wiped my face and looked at Malcolm.

"If I didn't leave you from death, I'm damn sure not leaving you for a whore hookup that happened before me."

Malcolm kissed me and told me he loved me more than I'd ever know. We both took a shot of tequila this time. I pulled my cell phone out and shared the recording of my visit to the hospital. He was beyond amused. Malcolm poured us another shot of tequila, and we made a toast. "To my wife, the love of my life who will fuck a bitch up on sight!" We took our shot and kissed. I then made a toast with another shot. "To the beautiful baby girl, I saw in the hospital today that is probably not my husband's. May she get to know her real daddy." We took the shot. That one hurt. By now, both of us were feeling the effects. Malcolm and I held each other for a while as we leaned on the bar. I licked and kissed his neck then removed my turtleneck. Malcolm used his teeth and kissed me, my neck and my breast through my bra. He unbuttoned and unzipped my jeans then lifted me up onto the bar and removed my boots. We managed to get my tight ass jeans off followed by my thong. Malcolm started kissing my toes and moved up my legs. His kisses felt so good. He gently kissed up my thighs and placed my legs on each of his shoulders.

"I love you, Mrs. Styles." He said as he retreated to my core and made love to me with his tongue and mouth until I was crying out his name repeatedly. The rest of the afternoon was spent holding on to each other under the covers where we physically communicated our love to each other like it was our last time.

The next day we had an appointment to look at two Midtown New York Penthouses. The first one was a little outdated but the views were perfect from the patio! The second penthouse was turnkey ready but didn't have a patio. The Realtor was so excited to get my number and email. She said she would be sending me properties, and she would definitely find the perfect penthouse for me and Malcolm. On our way to dinner, the attorney called Malcolm because the results had just come back. I was watching and listening the whole time. My heart was beating loud and fast. *"Yes. Really? What do I need to do now? Okay. Yes. No one else. Thank you. I will. Okay. Yes. Same to you. I will try it. Agreed. Merry Christmas!"*

He just sat there like I wasn't waiting to hear.

"Malcolm Xavier Styles, if you don't stop playing!"

He laughed. "You were right. It's not my baby!" My publicist will be putting out a statement ASAP on all media outlets that explain how a paternity test was taken, and I am not the father of ChanelDenero baby!" Malcolm kissed my hand and I kissed his.

"On sight." We both laughed!

That evening we had dinner at his dad's house. His home was not a mansion but it was a beautiful large two-story brick home. Malcolm's step-sisters joined us for dinner. They looked almost identical to their mom except one was really thin and one was not. That night we talked about so much. Dr. Styles asked me to please start calling him Pops. I was honored. I hugged him and said thank you. Malcolm found out that his dad visits his mom's grave at Christmas time and her birthday in May. He was shocked to hear that. Apparently, his dad was just there yesterday. We all just sat around and caught up like a typical family. That night when we left it was slightly emotional because of the newfound and rekindled relationships that had formed. I thanked Ms. Dorothy for the delicious dinner and hugged Papa Styles for a long time. His hugs reminded me of my dad. Malcolm and his dad said good-bye and made plans on seeing each other soon.

Chapter Thirty-Two

Malcolm

*H*er smile warmed my heart to levels I couldn't explain. I couldn't imagine my life without my Lexi. Me and Lexi cooked breakfast on Christmas morning and exchanged our gifts. I opened my gift first and was pleasantly surprised at the limited edition Rolex watch my baby gave me. I then gave her a medium box that housed a custom 40-carat diamond bracelet.

"Malcolm, Thank you!" She said as she kissed me with so much passion. We stripped down and went to the Jacuzzi. Just being in Lexi's presence, I was always ready to make love to her. I think about her constantly and watch her in admiration. The Christmas morning Jacuzzi was a memory that will forever be etched in my brain. Lexi had tears streaming down her cheeks as we made love. I knew without a doubt that she was my everything, and I was hers.

We had the best Christmas and New Year! Lexi and I were inseparable. I loved how she always had some part of her body on me. If she was standing by me, she had her arm around my waist or holding me from behind and biting on my back. If we were watching a movie, she was on my lap or had her feet on my chest. In the bed was another story. I loved everything about her and us. Lexi wore a dress on NYE that had me cussing in my head all night. I had to keep her on the dance floor to keep her close to me and away from everyone else. She wore a shimmering little dress that exposed her breast sides and her entire back. My name down her side made me smile. However, her succulent breasts were out and my smile vanished. Between the comments going around the AMS offices on how fine Lexi was and comments and articles on social media, I was trying not to kill someone. Looking at her watch the fireworks, I had to admit, I wasn't in pain anymore. Lexi came in my life and made me the happiest I have ever been. I admired her beauty. She had the prettiest face, body, legs, and feet. I'm one lucky man! I kissed her behind her ear.

~

*I*t was late, and I was headed home after a series of big meetings in New York all day. I just wanted to be home and in my huge bed with my beautiful wife. My mind was on my baby. I hated leaving her alone so much but this month we had a lot of negotiations and new artists coming out. In the last week, I might have seen her for a total of 8 hours. Tonight my plan was to snug in right behind her, make love to her and spend the next two days getting reacquainted.

When I walked into our bedroom, she was awake. Lexi had on this little tight nightgown. Lexi had a special glow on her. I could only pray that she was carrying my baby. I had plans but apparently, she had her own plans. Before I could protest, Lexi was placing me in her mouth and doing what she does to make me weak. "Oh hell!" I was about to lose it. Looking at her squatting and taking me in and out of her mouth was so fucking hot! With an unrecognizable voice, I spoke. "Baby, please I need to be inside of you quickly." I pleaded. She looked up and released me from her beautiful mouth. "You give me what I want and you can get what you want!" She said as she went right back to where she left off. Within minutes, I was giving my baby plenty of what she wanted. With my hand grabbing her hair, I kissed the fuck out of my wife then turned her around and showed her how much I missed her ass.

Chapter Thirty-Three

ALEXIS

My first Christmas as Mrs. Styles was by far my favorite! We had the house to ourselves, and we took advantage of it. I thought I couldn't love him any more than I already did. But spending these days and nights together at our home, just the two of us had me loving Malcolm to levels I didn't even know existed. On Christmas morning, we sipped hot tea and exchanged gifts as we sat on the floor by the tree and made love outside in our beautiful Jacuzzi. We enjoyed our home movie theater. We even played around in the studio. On New Year's Eve, we went to an AMS company party. Malcolm was just irresistible in every way. He probably thinks I am the definition of clingy. I had to laugh because it's true. I am when it comes to him, I loved every minute of being with my baby. After the year we had already experienced, I was looking forward to moving into a much better year. I looked over at Malcolm as we watched the fireworks and couldn't understand how he was so perfect for me.

After the holidays, Malcolm was working long hours and had to travel to NY on several occasions. To avoid having to stay the night, he usually left around 5 am and would return as late as midnight each time. He said he didn't like the thought of spending a night away from home. He was exhausted after those trips but I appreciated his sacrifice. One night when he returned home, I had a surprise for him. When Malcolm walked into the master bedroom. I was up. "What are you doing up, Babe?"

"Waiting on you, Babe."

He came over and kissed me. Between the intensity of the kiss and the infamous Malcolm groan, I knew what time it was.

"Baby, before we get going, I have a surprise for you." I took him by the hand and led him to the bathroom where I had the Jacuzzi tub full of water and several candles lit around it for him.

He smiled and started stripping down. "Why you not getting that little gown off?" He asked.

"This bath is for you. I'll be sitting right here while you relax tho." I replied.

He stood there, blinking. "I know for a fact you know I'm not getting in this tub without my fine ass wife."

"But baby, I want you to..."

Malcolm was standing in front of me pulling off my nightgown. "...I did this for you." I finished. As he went in for a kiss, I stopped him and said. "Baby, this is my night! You want me to please you while you stand, sit or lay?" The pupils in Malcolms eyes instantly went dark as he stared at me. Without waiting, I went down while he stood. As soon as I touched him, it was over. Hearing him let out a deep groan followed by a cuss word made me feel so turned on. I especially loved how quickly I could bring him to that point. My husband was a very blessed man and pleasing him required skills that I enjoyed showing off. He then showed me. Malcolm smacked my ass and said, "turn around and bend over, baby." I obliged and held on to the side of the tub as we called out each other's names and confessed our love for each other. We both soaked in the bubble bath and woke up in the afternoon the next day.

"Who knew I'd learn to love baths this much"

~

*J*n February, we returned home from a quick Valentine getaway, and I was sicker than I had ever been. After about 4 days of not being able to keep anything down and no appetite, we went to the doctor and found out I was pregnant. The doctor told us that I was already over 8 weeks pregnant. We were brought to tears with joy. Three weeks later, we found out I was pregnant with twins.

Malcolm wouldn't let me do anything. I cussed my husband out once because he canceled one of my hair appointments because he didn't want me leaning back to get my hair washed. Right after I cussed him out, I cried for the rest of the day. My hormones were out of control. If I wasn't tired, I was hungry. At any given moment I was being mean or balling my eyes out. I was always hot to the point of crazy especially, at night. Malcolm was amused and loved every moment of this. Me being pregnant didn't slow us down on the love making. We were just limited to our two to three manageable positions.

I designed the nursery and had it completed by a few of the contractors that helped me with the house. I went with a gender neutral theme of gray, white and gold. The room was adorable and fit for a prince or princess, two of them.

I had been trying to get Malcolm to commit to a birthday party, as his birthday was less than a month away. He was adamant about not having a birthday party. He did agree to a destination trip for the two of us. I already had a plan.

Chapter Thirty-Four

Birthdays

*L*exi was 4 months pregnant with our twins. She was growing and glowing! We landed in Aruba and were on a passenger boat to the exclusive island of Savaneta. The boat ride was only six miles from the Aruba airport. Lexi has been all secretive leading up to today and especially today. I was already happy and loved my gift! Anytime I can be with my baby uninterrupted, I was happy. We woke up early. Lexi had us matching birthday T-shirts. Mine said *Birthday Boy* on it and hers said *Birthday Boys Wife*! In our shorts and tennis shoes, we caught our flight very early and landed in Aruba a little afternoon. This was my birthday gift from her and I could already tell, I was going to enjoy these next 5 days, especially with my baby and those extra full breasts. As we approached the island, I could see the Aruba Ocean Villas. Once we reached the beachfront island, we were greeted by staff and escorted to one of the beautiful over the ocean villas. We went to the largest of about 10 all close to each other. The villa that Lexi had for us was open on all sides, with white curtains hanging. The villa had mahogany furniture throughout. The bed was huge and plush with large white pillows. I asked the island staffer about walls and he showed me how I could close them up if I wanted to. I already knew I would because Lexi could get real loud and vocal during lovemaking, and I was not about to have strangers whispering about us over the next several days. After showing us the custom chandeliers, huge soaking tub and beautiful ocean view he pointed us in the direction of the one restaurant that would serve us breakfast, lunch and dinner, the island pool and full bar. Lexi and I unpacked. She had to text family and friends to let them know we made it. I wanted to lay down but Lexi said she was starving, so we headed to the restaurant which was only a 5-minute walk away. As soon as we walked in, I heard *SURPRISE*! Boy was I surprised to be greeted by all of my friends wearing t-shirts that had my name and age on them! Servers were serving cocktails and appetizers. I could not believe she did this all without me knowing! Lexi had rented the island for me and my closest friends to celebrate my 34th birthday for the next 5 days. Twenty people, all expenses paid. She did this for me. I couldn't do anything but hug and kiss her "I love you so much." I told her as I kissed those lips. As the DJ started the music, I had to greet and hug everyone. My dad and Dorothy; Drew and Carla; Mr. and Mrs. Deveraux; Evelyn and Rich; Jess and her guy friend; Tebow and E'Marie; Big B and his female friend; Kim and her wife; DJTwist and his girlfriend. This birthday weekend was going to be epic! We spent the next five days eating, dancing, drinking, laughing, at the beach, in the pool, kayaking, jet skiing and snorkeling. This place was like paradise!

Chapter Thirty-Five

ALEXIS

*I*t was like old times! Me and my girls were having the best time! At 6 months pregnant, I was big as a house with these twins. Malcolm had arranged for the girls to spend a week with me for my 31st birthday. We laughed so hard reminiscing about Malcolm's birthday trip. We started with Jess' "flavor of the month" and his $120 he had for the entire trip and the fact that he said "must be nice " at least 2000 times over the duration of the trip. Then we moved to DJTwist's girlfriend having to be carried to her villa from the restaurant and the bonfire because she passed out from drinking. Or the infamous fall from the all-white dinner boat ride that most of the guys had to jump in and save her drunk ass! At the time it wasn't funny. We were all over it and pissed but now talking about it, we were in tears. We recapped those five days to include me crying hysterically and trying to run from a larger than life bug trying to attack me on the beach. The parents out drinking everyone and breaking it down on the dance floor every night! Carla bragged about reading four books on this trip and being so distant towards Drew most of the trip, Tebow's wife cursing him out in Spanish and Mrs. Deveraux packing a different wig for each day. The last night at the bonfire, Drew wore her Rick James wig and I thought I was going to go into labor from laughing.

On my actual birthday, Malcolm had the house decorated with 31 dozen of white roses and balloons. Drew flew in town to celebrate with us. That night he took us all to Charlie Palmer's Restaurant for my birthday dinner. I opened my gift and had a new purse. I loved it! It was all good until I was enlightened by Jess about the cost of my new Birkin bag. I dared not let on to Malcolm my disbelief but I wanted a drink so bad! I kissed him and said thank you! We all left the restaurant to head back to the house. That night they had a private birthday party for me. Evelyn was making everyone's drinks. I drank my water and sparkling cider. These guys were drinking and talking all types of shit! Malcolm had one drink, and he was one of the loudest. We turned the music up and danced and did a little karaoke. Don't ask me how and when but these drunks had changed into their swimsuits and were playing volleyball in the pool. I sat in my sports bra and shorts on the side of the pool and joined in the turn up!

The rest of the week, we enjoyed laying out at the pool almost every day and shopping. We ate a lot, stayed up late, shopped some more for the twins, got massages, and spa treatments. Evelyn shared with us that she and Rich were finally trying to get pregnant. She said the trip in Aruba must have changed him, and she was so excited. We were so happy for her. This birthday was very special and I couldn't be any happier!

Chapter Thirty-Six
Evelyn

A week in Las Vegas was just what the doctor ordered! I was so excited about spending time with Lex and Jess. I had not laughed as hard as I did this week for a long time. Being with Lexi and Jess was so therapeutic. I needed this trip and my best friends after the last few weeks that I'd had. Rich has always been needy but lately his needy has been mixed with baby momma drama. Honestly, I can just about deal with anything but this ghetto shit just wasn't my thing! We're supposed to be working on making a baby, and he's more concerned about his ex not giving him her new address. For the last two weeks, he hasn't touched me. When I brought it to his attention right before I left, he apologized and said it's because he's stressed. In my mind, I thought *you broke motherfucker! Stressed? I've been stressed since I took you back against my family's wishes even with your two-year-old and no job. Stressed? How about I'm stressed because you have had 5 jobs in the last three years. You won't even help me clean, cook, grocery shop, or get gas in my car, without me asking you. On a scale from 1 to 10, sex with you is a 4! Stressed? I can't work my 12 hour shift at the hospital without you calling or texting me all day about something. Where is the ketchup? What are you going to eat for dinner? How much dog food goes in the bowl? Damn! I want kids more than anything. You finally agreed to give me that and now you're stressed behind your ex, and we can't fuck! Fuck you!* Instead of saying what I was feeling, I just walked away and started packing my bags for Vegas.

My flight back home was bitter-sweet. I'm sitting on my flight, tired as hell. I was happy to be returning home to Rich. I know now that I just needed time away. He was my first and only love. He was also my husband and I married him knowing all his imperfections. I think being around Lexi and Malcolm put things in perspective for me. I'm sure being around them made everyone want what they have. Lexi was the happiest. I have never seen her so happy and complete. Even with her huge stomach, she looked radiant. Her smile and laugh were contagious and her energy was even better. The way Malcolm loves and attends to Lexi is beyond beautiful. After her birthday dinner last night, we all partied it up at the house. Drew had shown up and was a part of the festivities for a couple of days. That's a whole nother story because who is he and Jess thinking they're fooling? Anyway, I served up drinks all night, and we cut up! The dance/karaoke contest was the best. Lexi and Malcolm were just nasty dancing to everything! She was twerking with that big stomach, and he was thrusting and pumping was just too much! It wasn't as bad when they were dancing on the fast songs, but seriously, how can you dance like that off John Legend song *Another Again? Just ghetto!* Jess and I performed Salt and Pepper. We started with *Tramp* and ended with *Chick on the side*. This night was a blast. We all ended up playing volleyball in the pool, and we continued to drink. I was partnered with Malcolm, and we played against Jess and Drew. Lexi just sat on the side and distracted my partner. Needless to say, Jess and Drew were winning. Every time they scored a point they hugged! They weren't that damn happy! I finally got out of the pool after my partner went to the side of the pool and started kissing on the cheerleader's stomach. I made another round of drinks and after a while, Malcolm and Lexi had gone in for the night. I sat and talked with Jess and Drew until about 1 am and left them to get some rest before my flight in a few hours. I was thankful for the friends that I considered family. I was also thankful for my family.

Chapter Thirty-Seven

ALEXIS

The baby shower was on July 5th at our home. Dre, Jess and Evelyn were the hosts. This baby shower was grandiose. They left no stone unturned. We had everyone there but Michelle and Barack. There were so many big names from the music industry considering that the first heirs to the AMS Music label were coming. I was just overwhelmed. Pops, Ms. Dorothy and Malcolm's step sisters were there. Evelyn's husband, Rich, came with her. I had a few friends from my job there. We had packages coming in daily for our twins. We were so blessed.

On July 24th, we welcomed our twins, Malcolm III and Ana Lynn. Perfection was an understatement. Baby Malcolm had his dad's and his grandfather's eyes. He had my mouth and smile. Miss Ana was already a little lady. She looked like a perfect mix of me and Malcolm. I often found myself staring at them for hours when they were asleep. I started back singing. I sang to them as much as I could. They seem to love it. Having twins is not for the weak. We were constantly adhering to one or both of their needs around the clock. Ms. Rita was heaven sent and helped tremendously with the twins. She would often let me get some rest by taking care of them first thing in the morning. Malcolm was amazing too. He was up several times through the night feeding and changing them. Sometimes he would leave for work with less than 3 hours of sleep. It was nice seeing him so vulnerable and hands on. I fell even more in love with him. Although we were tired every day, we loved being parents.

Malcolm accompanied me to my six week check-up on a Friday morning. The doctor told me I was doing great and could resume activities. He even set up an appointment and gave me plenty of materials to read to choose the right birth control for us. My appointment was in a few weeks. Malcolm and I couldn't get home fast enough. I really missed my husband. Malcolm and I were in the shower getting my hair curly again, within 10 minutes after arriving home. Malcolm was gripping my ass as he had me lifted and up against the shower wall. I'm sure they're bruises from his hands to match the nail marks on his back and bite marks on his face, neck and shoulder. Life was good. When I went to get on my birth control four weeks later, I was informed that I was pregnant again.

Chapter Thirty-Eight

Malcolm

I was fearful that Lexi and I wouldn't be able to conceive after the shooting and miscarriage. Finding out that we were expecting for the first time was a feeling I'll never be able to put in words. My heart was at its fullest. By the time we made it to see a doctor, Lexi was already two months pregnant. We held each other and I let her cry her tears of joy. Fighting back my tears, I thanked God for answering my prayers.

We had a baby shower that was nothing short of over the top. We had gifts that would last for up to 5 years. Our twins couldn't get here soon enough. Lexi's stomach was huge but man she was beautiful! I teased her every chance I got. After the baby shower, me, Lexi, Jess, Drew, my dad, Dorothy, Tebow and his wife, Big B and his new girlfriend, Evelyn and her husband stayed up talking, laughing and sitting out by the pool. They were drinking and a few of them were swimming. The feeling of love was all around us. It was good having house guests. That night after making love to my wife, I went downstairs to make sure we turned the pool lights off. On my way back upstairs, I heard moaning. I then heard a female say Drew's name! "That boy is wild!" I laughed it off as I shook my head and went to bed.

The next morning, we had a huge breakfast in our outdoor

kitchen. A few of our family and friends were leaving to catch their flights. We hugged and said our goodbyes. Saying bye to my dad was getting harder because we were getting so close. We talked at least once a day on the phone. Always having plenty to talk about. He even came out one weekend about a month ago, and we played golf. After seeing our guest off, we went back into the house. We had a couple more house guests that hadn't left yet. Lexi went into the kitchen where Drew was and got her a bottle of water and went to sit on the couch.

"Drew how was your night?" I asked.

He stopped chewing and looked like he was busted. He had a nervous laugh. "Man! Y'all don't mind if I stay until later tonight do you?"

"I love it! You can stay the entire weekend!" Lexi exclaimed, all excited from the sofa.

About two hours later, Jess came to the family room. Lexi and I both looked at her then looked at each other.

About 3 weeks later Lexi went into labor. We had just finished watching a movie in the home theater. We just finished eating chicken wings, fries and ice cream. As soon as I helped her up from her seat, her water broke.

At the hospital, she was like I'd ever seen her. I hated to admit it but Lexi was a *psychopath* in that room. In between contractions, Lexi said some horrible things. Every other word was a cuss word. "Where the fuck is the doctor? What the fuck are we watching? Fuck this. Fuck that. Why the fuck aren't y'all helping me? Don't give me another fucking compliment!" Then she turned on me. "You did this shit to me! I'm so fucking mad at you, Malcolm! If you ever leave me, I'm going to kill your black ass!" Then she switched up and started crying. "I love you, Malcolm." "I'm sorry." "Do you still love me?"

After 10 hours of labor, Malcolm Xavier Styles III and Ana Lynn Styles were here! Lexi and I both were emotionally happy. We couldn't believe we had a son and a daughter. I'm not sure about other babies but the newest Styles were the most beautiful babies I'd ever seen.

I was home as much as I could to help with the twins. Trey was always hungry and always crying. Ana was the complete opposite. We had to wake her up most of the time to eat and all she did was sleep and smile. Lexi was a perfect mom! She along with Ms. Rita had gotten into a routine. I was the automatic storyteller every night after their baths. Most nights I was up with the twins to let Lexi rest. I went with Lexi to her 6 week post appointment. We used this outing like a date. We stopped and got coffee before the appointment. Did our infamous seat dancing to every song that played in the car and kissed on hands and fingers. The doctor told Lexi she was doing great. He couldn't believe she had lost her baby weight so fast. We had agreed on birth control that would give us a couple of years before we had another baby.

When we returned from our appointment, Ms. Rita told us the babies had just laid down and fell asleep. We couldn't get to the room quick enough. I suggested we go into the shower so no one could hear. I already knew Lexi screams would wake up the babies in the next room. If you asked her, she would say, it's my moans and grunts. I missed my baby so much!

Eleven months later, our Son Mase was here. His full name was Mason Andrew Styles. I named him after Drew, my best friend. Having Mase was much easier than the twins. Lexi was in labor for a total of 4 hours. He came out strong and beautiful. Lexi just kissed him continuously. He was just like his big brother, always clinging to his mom's breast for milk. Lexi might have held Mase a little too much because he was already spoiled by her instantly. He would only stop crying if Lexi held him. *They both cried all the time.*

Chapter Thirty-Nine

ALEXIS

Not even a year later on June 14th, we welcomed our son. Mason Andrew, our Mase. He was the most beautiful boy. His eyes were so bright. He was very aware of things going on around him. I found myself holding him a lot more than I should have. His big brother and big sister loved him too.

After having Mase, I felt myself slowly changing. Within a week or so after giving birth to my third child, I went through a depression state for several weeks. I cried all the time. I cried because he was perfect and beautiful, I cried because my family was a dream come true. I cried because Malcolm was so supportive and the best husband. I cried because I was a baby machine. I cried because I was tired of being pregnant. I cried because I was tired of breast-feeding. I never ate a real meal. I was losing weight too fast. My hair stayed in a messy bun or ponytail. I hardly left the house. I was so afraid of getting pregnant again in six weeks. I hoped I wouldn't be one of those women that just stayed barefoot and pregnant. I missed my old life and my old body. I felt worthless. Crying was the only thing that made sense.

These last six weeks have been tough on me and Malcolm's relationship. I was pushing him away and didn't know how not to. The only thing that made sense or felt normal was to cry. I knew

Malcolm was my weakness. I also knew deep down that he was my strength. When Mase was delivered, Malcolm kissed me and told me that he was so happy, and then he said, "I want to have a house full of babies with you." I didn't know how to tell him that I wanted a break. Everyone including him was so happy about our family growing and expressed it openly and often. The birth of our new edition was on every social media outlet. I could feel myself going to a familiar place of isolation. I soon found myself avoiding my husband. I was afraid to talk with him fearing the conversation of how much we craved each other or him expressing how he couldn't wait to be inside of me again. It was like I didn't want him to even want me. I didn't understand why I took it to the level of extreme that I did. I never fixed myself up, I didn't sit next to him. I wouldn't even leave the house. Malcolm had arranged a very romantic lunch for us one day in the rose garden on the property and I didn't even go. I saw the set up from the office window and cried my eyes out. The whole scene was so beautiful and looked like it was out of a magazine. Malcolm looked just as beautiful. I couldn't bring myself to get pretty like he asked. I couldn't enjoy the beautiful Summer day. I couldn't risk getting intimate or consumed with wanting him. I didn't want any type of intimacy. I didn't want to feel happy. That night, I closed myself in a guest room and in the dark, had a break-down and cried myself to sleep. I avoided being in our bed as often as possible. I was spending a lot of time in the nursery or our home gym on the treadmill. Malcolm was always trying to talk with me but I always said I was good and avoided him. I loved Malcolm. Malcolm loved me. I realized that I mostly cried because I was hurting him. I was losing my mind and couldn't understand how I let myself hurt my best friend. I felt his warmth and energy every time he kissed me. I could also feel his heartache. I went to my post check-up appointment by myself. I didn't tell Malcolm because I knew if he went, there was a strong possibility that we would end up pregnant again. The morning he found out, broke me because I broke him. When Malcolm left the house that day, I prayed to God to please help me.

Chapter Forty
Malcolm

We returned home and everything was good, so I thought. I assumed it was because she was tired as to why she wasn't herself. In the beginning, Lexi would kiss me on my cheek each morning. As the days went on, she would comply and give me a quick peck on my lips, only after I stood in front of her and invaded her space. At first, I thought she was playing around and being sassy until I noticed she really was looking annoyed. The kiss before I left the house and the kiss when I got home was completely forced. I didn't know how to handle any of this. I have never felt rejection and never thought I would from her. I tried to ask her what was going on? *Nothing.* Is what she always replied. I made plans and always had to cancel because she always had a reason for not being able to do anything. I even set up a beautiful picnic in her rose garden. It was everything she loved... My Lexi would have loved this. This Lexi informed me through text that she had a migraine and had to lay down. She asked if we could reschedule. She hadn't shared a shower with me since she gave birth. She hardly ever smiled and I even noticed her eyes had lost that beautiful sparkle that could light up a room. She looked sad all the time. I was lost. I didn't know what to do or what was going on with my baby.

The next morning, I woke up in our bed alone. This was becoming more frequent over the last couple of weeks. My heart was breaking into a million pieces. *It feels like she has stopped loving me.* I showered and got dressed. As I exited the bedroom, Lexi was coming up the stairs carrying a cup of tea. Even in her robe and headscarf, she was still the most beautiful woman to me. *I needed a hug from her like I need air to breathe.*

"Good morning, Love" I greeted her. "Good morning", she replied as she looked at me quickly and looked back down.

"Baby, when is your appointment?" I stopped her from walking past me. "I would love to go with you," I said to her.

"It was yesterday." as she walked off.

I followed her. "Lexi, why wouldn't you tell me?" I was visibly upset and disappointed. "Don't walk away from me!" I yelled.

Without even looking at me. "Malcolm, I need to check on the babies. Maybe we can talk later."

"Later? Just answer the question, Lexi!" She just looked up and into my eyes, never saying anything. A tear fell from Lexi's eye. I went to her and put my arms around her. "Talk to me, baby." I kissed her lips.

She tensed up. "Please, Malcolm just give me time?"

She walked into the nursery. I turned around, walked down the stairs and out the door. *My world felt fucked up.* I couldn't understand what to do or what was happening. A tear fell from my eye as I threw my shades on a got in the sports car and drove off.

I went to my office and was happy that Drew was in town for a day or two. He immediately knew something was wrong and admitted that he noticed a couple of weeks ago. Drew and I went to lunch and talked for over 2 hours. I didn't realize how much I missed our conversations and catching up. I shared with him everything that had been going on or not between Lexi and I. When we returned to AMS-WEST, we participated in a few meetings and met with a few executives. The team ordered a late dinner and I had a chance to catch a newly signed hip hop trio group work on their first project. They were very happy to see Drew and I in the studio with them. We caught up for a few minutes but soon left after a couple of women hanging out in the room were taking pictures and wanted a picture with each of us. I knew all too well how this scenario played out and was the first to exit. Drew and I spent well into the night talking more. He shared with me that he and Jess have been developing a special friendship. "What does that mean, Drew?" I asked.

"It means Lexi has no idea and Jess isn't ready to tell her or anyone," Drew said. I just stared at him as I thought back to all the times they were together.

"Wait! Lexi doesn't know?"

Drew looked serious, "Black, your wife knows nothing about me and Jess or our secret."

He smiled. "Jess is very private and I like that about her. "I told you because it doesn't sit well with me to keep shit from you. That's not how we roll. You will always be the one to know where all the bodies are buried." He stated. We bumped fists and at the same time said, "4 life!" This was something we had between us since we became friends in college. Drew told me way more than I really wanted to know about him and Jess. He also told me that Lexi had shut down her conversations with Jess and Evelyn as well. He told me that Jess was really concerned and believed Lexi was going through postpartum depression. We both looked it up online and agreed. He also told me that he received a text from Jess about two hours ago. He said that Jess' text stated that Lexi reached out to her and was crying hysterically because she felt you were going to leave her.

I immediately dabbed Drew and left. The entire drive home, I thought about Lexi. I reminisced about her sleeping on the plane when I first met her to the vows we took and made to each other. I thought about her laugh and her tears. Postpartum depression was a real thing and I needed to get Lexi the help she needs. I just want to hold her and let her know that I loved her more than I loved myself. *There was only one way I would leave her and that is the day I leave this earth.*

Chapter Forty-One

ALEXIS

Malcolm came home late that night. He didn't even take off his clothes before he climbed into the bed. He hugged me from behind so close. His arms felt so good around me. He whispered he loved me and the tears fell like water on my pillow. He immediately could tell I was awake and crying.

"Alexis, please talk to me." He was kissing my face and earlobe.

"I'm scared," I whispered.

Malcolm turned on the light. He turned me over. "I need to see your face." I turned over. He placed his face right above mine and started rubbing my hair and face. "Tell me what it is that you're scared of?" I couldn't formulate my words because of my emotions and tears. Malcolm started kissing my tears, face and lips. He looked like he wanted to cry. "Talk to me, baby. Tell me everything. Tell me what you need. Tell me why you're crying"

Through my tears, "I haven't been honest with you." I managed to say. "I have been depressed and it's not the first time I've suffered from depression. I'm afraid that you're going to leave me because I am a mess and I don't want any more kids right now."

"Why wouldn't you tell me this, Lexi? Babe, are you serious?"

"I never wanted to hurt you," I said through my tears.

"You hurt me by avoiding me. You hurt me by not loving me."

He kissed my nose. "Lexi, you hurt me by confiding in your friends instead of me."

"Are you going to leave me?" I asked. "Please don't," I cried.

"I'm so sorry baby." I sat up. I covered my face with my hands and started crying more.

"Come here, Baby," Malcolm pulled me to him and held me like a baby. He let me cry as he rubbed and hugged me.

"First of all, I would never leave you. Second, let's get on birth control, okay?" Malcolm asked. "When you're ready for more kids, you just let me know?" Malcolm lifted my chin, "I love the ground you walk on baby and I need you in every way." We kissed for the first time in over 6 weeks using our tongues. Kissing Malcolm was like medicine. With every second our tongues being entangled, I felt my strength slowly return. We made love without actual penetration. It was a beautiful night and without a doubt, if I had made love to my husband, with him inside of me, I would have gotten pregnant, with another set of twins or triplets.

The next day we were at the doctors' office getting on birth control. We even made an appointment with my therapist for the following week. We had to wait another week before we could make love. Malcolm made reservations for a weekend getaway and the level of reconnecting we shared made our bond even stronger.

Chapter Forty-Two

Malcolm & Alexis

*I*t was close to midnight and I couldn't sleep. I decided to throw on some workout clothes and head down to the home gym. I stopped to check in on the kids on my way down to workout. Trey and Ana had just turned 3 and Mase had just turned 2. They were sleeping soundly. Lexi left yesterday morning for a photoshoot in New York. Me and the kids would be flying out tomorrow to join her. In the last couple of years, Lexi had begun modeling for top fashion designers. It all started with pictures of her and I on social media. She received hundreds of comments about her body, outfits and her style. She then started getting clothes sent to the house for her to wear and promote the different designers. The cameras as well as the designers loved my wife! She had already been a guest on a couple of talk shows and started taking pictures for magazines and even landed on a huge marquee for the Wynn Hotels promoting high-end stores like Prada, Gucci, Valentino and Tom Ford. Lexi was juggling being a full-time mom and a sought after model. By now, with the three kids, we had two nannies'. Lexi and I had just returned from a 10-day trip to Paris. We were fortunate enough to travel with all three kids and the nannies. If I had to choose a new place to live, Paris would be my choice. Lexi and I fell in love yet again while in Paris. Those memories will forever be etched in my heart.

I placed my ear pods in my ear and started running on the treadmill as I listened to songs that reminded me of my wife. I hated being apart from her. This was the second night without her home. My mind went back over the last three years married to Lexi. Our kids were our life. Lexi finally resigned from her job. I wasn't spending countless hours at the music label like I used to. We had hired top executives to pretty much handle the day to day operations at the music label. Lexi, the kids and myself traveled between the Las Vegas main house and our New York penthouse. The penthouse was off 57th street in New York, NY. We purchased a 6,234 sq ft two story with 5 bedrooms and 5 bathrooms. You enter through a private elevator into a gracious foyer. The views of central park and the Hudson River through the ceiling to floor windows made this place spectacular. I owe this one to Lexi. She found it, and we both fell in love with it. In these last couple of years, we have traveled all over the world and enjoyed every bit of it. The best part of our trips was when we could have the kids with us. Their personalities were already different. Trey was a miniature me. He had all of my mannerisms. The way he walked and the way he looked just like me was crazy. He was so affectionate and fun. He was also the most serious one. He would spend all day building things and asking questions. Ana was a daddy's girl to the core. She looked a lot like her mom, but she wanted to do everything I did. Whatever I ate, she wanted the same thing. Wherever I sat down, she was right there next to me. In the swimming pool, I was her personal gym. She and her mom loved shopping and Lexi always kept her looking like a little model. Now our baby boy was something different. Mase was strictly about his momma. He looked a lot like me, but he interacted with me the least. I usually had my time with him and Trey when I took them to their barber. We had started a tradition of hanging out after their haircuts and finishing with ice cream. Mase really enjoyed being read to and oddly he loved watching the news. I am not sure what he understood while watching the news but it kept him engaged. He was happy and content as long as he had his eyes on his mom. If she left the room, all hell broke loose. They were all different variations of us.

It was the first of November, and I was looking forward to spending the month in New York with our family. We were hosting Thanksgiving this year and had invited everyone to dinner at our home. Drew and his parents, Jess and her parents, Evelyn and her husband, Tebow and his family, Big B and at least 4 more guests. We were planning a dinner for over 30 people. We had a lot to be thankful for and I couldn't wait. Lexi had shared with me in Paris that she would like to get information on her birth parents. She cried as she talked about it. I told her I would help her. I already had someone on it. I was waiting until we made it to New York before I informed her of the information we had.

My phone rang. It was Lexi and it was after 3 am on the east coast. "Hey baby, is everything okay?" I asked as soon as I answered. "Hi baby, did I wake you?" she asked. "I couldn't sleep. What's wrong? Why are you up?" I asked. I turned off the treadmill and grabbed a towel. I then went and sat on a weight bench. "Malcolm, please let me come home in the morning and fly back with you and the kids? I don't want you and the kids to fly here without me." Lexi shared. "I understand and I know why you feel the way you feel. Of course, baby." I replied. "Thank you, Malcolm. My heart couldn't take it if something happened to you and the kids." She stated. "I know." I understood everything Lexi was feeling. We had discussed in many therapy sessions over the last two years her fear of losing everyone in her family again. The traumatic experience of losing the only family she had was the reason for her episodes of depression and feelings of loneliness. "I'll call Kim now and get you on the first flight out in the morning. I love you, baby." I said. Lexi told me that she loved me, and we ended the call.

I picked her up at the passenger pick up around 11:30 am later that morning. As soon as I saw her, my heart lit up. She was my everything. I exited the driver's side of the Bentley and opened my arms for her. Lexi walked up quickly and I picked her up. We hugged and kissed then I put her down. I opened her door and made sure she was inside and I got in on my side and drove off.

Driving home holding hands, I thought about this being the best feeling. My baby would always be my baby.

"Where're my babies?" Lexi shouted as soon as she hit the front entrance of our home. *"Mommy Mommy!"* The kids shouted as they came running from around a corner and down the hallway to the foyer. The smiles on their faces were priceless! Trey was leading the pack. He reached his momma first, smiling from ear to ear. Ana was right on his heels. When she made it to her mom, she pushed him away from her mom and the fight was on. Lexi broke up the fight and began kissing them both all over their faces. They were in heaven and kissing her back. We then heard screams and cries coming towards us. Mase came walking towards her crying uncontrollably. The way he was crying, you would have thought his whole world was over. Without a doubt, he loved his mom beyond normal. Lexi picked him up and kissed him. All of a sudden he stopped. My heart was full.

That night after the kids went to bed, Lexi and I resorted to our bedroom. That night we made love damn near all night. The way our lips and bodies loved each other was unbelievable. We kissed and made love like we could not get enough of each other. Our lovemaking sessions were always on another level of exquisite, but something was different this time. That night alone, Lexi had at least four explosive orgasms and I was in a trance each time. I watched her silhouette from the moonlight coming through our glass walls and listened to her sounds of love, as she was on top of me. Watching her was mind blowing and I couldn't explain the feeling I was feeling in the moment. I pulled her off me and brought her up to my face. Lexi didn't last two minutes. We layed in each other's arms and confessed our love. We all flew out the following morning.

～

The following week, Essence Magazine did a story on our family for the Thanksgiving Edition. We were interviewed in our penthouse in New York. They took several pictures of the family and the house. They did several with just the two of us and just as many with us and the kids. As the nannies got the kids, the photographer asked us to look natural and show our love and admiration for each other. I had soon forgotten the cameras were there because looking at my beautiful husband had me in another space. The space that only he could get me too. Malcolm had his arms around my waist and whispered in my ear "I'm starving." I'm sure I was blushing, as I giggled. I whispered in his ear "I'm ready for another baby." He pulled back to look at me, "Are you telling me the truth?" He asked. I shook my head to say yes. Malcolm placed his mouth on my mouth and we kissed. I moaned. He moaned. We heard several shutter clicks as the camera took pictures. Then we heard, "Are you guys ready for the interview to start?"

During the interview, we sat on the sofa and held hands.

How did you two meet? We both smiled. "We met at the airport." He said. "Actually, we met on the airplane after he got the flight attendant to get me to sit next to him on our flight to Las Vegas." I clarified. We laughed remembering that day. "We haven't parted since that day," Malcolm added as we looked at each other, and he kissed my hand.

How did you know Lexi was the one for you? And Malcolm for you? "I knew Malcolm was the one when he buckled my seatbelt on the airplane. I thought that was the sweetest thing to me." "I knew Lexi was the one when she first kissed me and I never wanted her to stop."

What's the most attractive feature about each other? "Her smile." "His eyes"

How is life now that you have a family? "Trey, Ana and Mase are our life. We feel complete and Blessed." Malcolm answered. "My family is a dream come true. I'm the happiest, I've ever been." I answered.

"What keeps you two in love? "Love. I make love to my wife every day. Even if it's not through the physical act, it's in my words or actions."

"Commitment. Being apart is not an option. God gave us each other as a gift and a gift from God is never to be unappreciated or damaged."

"What do you two like to do for fun?" We both smiled. We couldn't tell the world our favorite hobby. "We love listening to music. I dance and sing for him all the time." I said. "We also love to kiss. I could kiss my baby 24/7 and never get tired." Malcolm said as he's looking at me licking his lips.

Cover of magazine-Malcolm 36, Lexi 34, Malcolm 3, Ana 3, Mason 2, and *(Twin boys in Lexi's stomach)*

Epilogue

Drew

I should have known better! Why did I bring Carla to Aruba for five days? We've been dating for about two years now. However, we started having issues a little after six months of dating. She hates my lifestyle and wanted a commitment from me. I made it clear that I wasn't ready for any of that. She made like she was okay at first, but she never was. Her weekend visits always ended with her crying and me irritated as fuck. It was always the same conversation.

We were leaving Aruba first thing in the morning and I couldn't wait to get as far away from her as I could. Sitting on the shore of this beautiful island was very peaceful and romantic. It was close to 2 am. I was enjoying looking at the beautiful night sky while listening to the water waves. It was therapeutic as I thought about my life and relationships. Carla and I have been fighting since the first day here and tonight things hit an all time high. She called me a "scared bitch" and I was very close to disrespecting her. Instead, I left the villa. I brought her here to celebrate my best friend, Malcolm's birthday. His wife Lexi paid for all of us to fly and stay here to surprise him for his birthday. I even thought for a second that we just might bond since we're here with all couples to include my parents who like her. Well, they did. My mom has asked me a couple of times while on this trip about what's going on with Carla? She even said, "If that little bitch keeps mistreating you, I'm going to snatch a knot in her little ass!" I told my mom not to worry. She is just going through something. My dad wasn't saying anything, which said a lot. Being their only child, my parents were very protective. Tonight, Carla crossed the line. She asked me if I loved her and I said "I think I do" and things went even further down.

When I first met Carla, I thought she could be the one. Carla was very pretty and had a great shape. She was multiracial and independent. I had received an invitation to the grand opening of her beauty bar. We were introduced by a mutual friend and went out about a week after that. She was sweet and attractive. After a couple of months of spending time together and inviting her to a lot of events with me, I knew she was not the one. She soon started asking me about every female that was a female. No matter what I said, she assumed I was lying and every time I said I wasn't ready for a committed relationship, she said it was because of my other women. Every outing and each time we spent time together, we'd end up in an argument.

I heard footsteps and turned around. To my pleasure, I saw Jess walking toward me. I stood up as she approached me. "What are you doing out here?" I asked. "I came to check on you. What the hell are you doing out here?" She replied. "Naomi, you something else." I laughed. "Shut up!" she said as she laughed. When I first met Jess at the hospital, and she turned around, I thought to myself that she looked like a young Naomi Campbell. Her beautiful dark complexion and full mouth were sexy as hell. Jess was built like a gymnast and wore her hair in long braids all the time. We had started talking on the phone weekly about 2 months ago. I was surprised at how easy our conversations evolved. We both sat back down on my blanket. I smiled to myself, knowing that she came to check on me. "I can't believe you walked down here without some drinks!" I said as I threw a pebble toward the water. She replied "I'm mad at myself too. Shit." Without looking at me, Jess spoke in a serious tone, "She's not the one for you, Drew." "I don't know why you didn't just come with me," I replied. "I should have because this ninja has annoyed the hell out of me." We both laughed. "Are you still thinking about coming to Savannah soon to visit?" Jess asked. "You just tell me when you want me there and I'm there," I replied. We both turned our heads at the same time to look at each other as our hands discreetly found each other on the blanket.

~

*T*he funeral was being covered on a couple of news stations and had all sorts of politicians and prominent people in attendance. My mom showed very little emotion burying the man she had been married to for the last 37 years. Me and my two older brothers took care of everything and made sure we acknowledged the hundreds of guests that came to show their respect for our father, Senator Howard Holmes. It was the day after Christmas and this had been the saddest holiday in the Holmes household ever.

A few days after the memorial service, the attorney called us in to read our fathers will. We were all very nervous, especially our mother. In attendance for the reading was; Mother, Alberta Holmes; myself, the youngest son, Howard II; Herbert and his wife, Gina; Albert, the youngest twin; and my aunt Peggy, our mother's older sister. The lead attorney read a letter written by my dad.

My dearest family,

I hope everyone is okay. Please know that I love each of you and will always watch over you. My family has been my backbone and my motivation. Every-thing I have done, I did for you. All that I have is left for you all. My lovely wife, Alberta, I pray that you forgive me for any hurt I have caused you. I hope you know that I love you and have always loved you. Please promise that you'll make things right and share my love. You know what I'm talking about. To my children, my assets have been split amongst you all. Please be strong for your mom and know that I love you with all my heart.

While I was alive I held a secret for over 30 years. Now that I am deceased, the truth needs to be told. All I ask is that you all forgive me. I have a safe deposit box at the Bank of California. Paperwork has already been signed for you all to have access to it. The only condition is that all three of my sons have to be together. Inside the safe deposit box, you will find information on your little sister who at the time I wrote this letter turned 30. You have a sister named Alexis Lynn. Please find her. Me and your mom had to make the hardest decision of our lives. I'm sorry. I hope and pray one day you understand. I will let your mom explain it when she's ready. Alexis was last living in Las Vegas. The last time we saw her she was leaving her biological parent's funeral. She was 19 then. In the safe deposit box are pictures of Alexis from birth and every year afterward until she turned 18. Please tell her all the good things about me. Please tell her that I prayed every night for her to be safe and find love. Please tell her that I've always loved her too. I also left her 25% of all that I have obtained. My tears are falling as I'm writing this letter to you all. I hope I was a good husband and a good dad to you. I love you forever.

Dad

Herbert Holmes, Esq

~

Two weeks later...

Man she's beautiful! Same face and features as all of us. I will finally meet my little sister. I placed the picture back in my wallet. I jumped in my Lyft with my bags and headed to the Las Vegas MGM, where I would be staying for a while.

CPSIA information can be obtained
at www.ICGtesting.com
Printed in the USA
LVHW092036061120
670968LV00007B/1059